For Alexandra
Love
[signature] x

KEEPING IT
SEMPER FI

— • —

WHEN GOD TAKES A SIDE PERCEPTION
BOOK 3

DAVID PARKER-ROSS

TAIRIS ANDERS MEDIA

Facebook.com/DavidParkerRoss

Contact@JennaPlural.com

Keeping It Semper Fi © 2023 David Parker Ross

First Edition May 2022

Dedication

For the world's greatest nephew

Jaxson Collins

Buddy, as I write this dedication, you are not yet one year old, and we have not even met in person. But your amazing smile brightens my day, and I look forward to every time your parents post pictures of you.

Right now, this book means little more to you than something interesting to chew on. Indeed due to its content, you really should be an adult before trying to read it. By that time, I will be extremely old and senile or dead. So I wanted to say do not be confused about why I dedicated a book to you about a psychotic serial killer. It was simply the book I wrote the year this world saw your arrival.

All my love goes with you, Jaxson, on your journey through this crazy thing called life.

Uncle David
22nd October 2022

AUTHOR'S NOTE

Perceptions is a series that tells tales from different characters' perspectives. Each has their own ideas, their own values, their own beliefs, and their own memories.

The characters, including the narrator, have their own perception of the events that took place at the time of the stories. They may very well have political, religious, and social opinions. Those opinions do not necessarily reflect this author or anyone involved with the creation of this work. Indeed I have very much tried to keep my personal opinions out of the stories.

The whole idea is to leave it to you, the reader, to make up your mind on the rights and wrongs of the characters within the tales.

Memory is a fickle beast; not everyone will remember events similarly. One should not assume that a narrator is either accurate or, for that matter, even truthful.

Perceptions... It's all about who you believe.

Clear Skies to You,
David Parker-Ross

KEEPING IT SEMPER FI

BY EMMA DODGSON

Dedication
Jenna Plural
My heart, my soul, my leader

From the private files of Lieutenant Emma Dodgson (Deceased)

If you are reading this, then I am dead.

It was never intended to be read in my lifetime, and I have no idea if anyone will ever read it. It is not because I am ashamed of anything, far from it. I am a proud American patriot and did what I saw as necessary for my country and my leader, Jenna Plural.

I realize that others may not see my acts in the same light. Therefore, it will remain locked in an encrypted file only to be accessed upon the recording of my death.

I recently finished reading Mr. Phelkar's account of the rise of Jenna Plural, in which I was honored that he spoke of how he met me. He is such a precious and kind man. However, he neglected to mention the special intimate time we spent together. I am sure he is just being a gentleman.

I also read the account by that foul-mouthed Australian Jezebel. Oh, how it irks me how she wormed her way into Mr. Phelkar's kind heart. She claims to have shed tears, but I know a crocodile when I see one.

I thought it would be fun and interesting to write my account of events. Though I doubt anyone would be as interested in my thoughts and opinions as they are in Mr. Phelkar's.

I do not know how this will turn out as I'm not as well educated as him, and frankly, I have never written anything before in my entire life.

One thing I must discuss before I begin. Mr. Phelkar and Stacey Grant are clearly under the idea that I am shy and reserved. I don't think I am. I am, however, frequently uncomfortable speaking to people. They make several references to my speech impediment. I have a very pronounced stutter.

This resulted from a brain injury I incurred when I was seven, and my father threw me against the mantlepiece in our living room. It may have been prevented had they sought medical attention at the time, but the damage became permanent and incurable. Although it has been a big part of my life, it has no place in this story.

I am not about to give this account and include something that annoys me even more than it would you were I were to do so. If it gives you some solace to imagine my stuttering and stammering, then, by all means, go ahead. However, I have no intention of placating anyone who expects to read or hear my difficulties in conversation.

My story begins in my hometown of Sedona, Arizona, and I joined the United States Marines straight out of high school. I did not have the grades for college, so military service was the only option available to me. Having said that, the marines are the only division of the military that you cannot be called up for and must apply. I did. I applied three times before I was accepted. I am not exactly an athlete, I'm small and appear ineffectual in most people's eyes, and it was quite a struggle to get through the physical rigors of the selection process. To my surprise and probably everyone else, I finally managed it, and my first and last assignment as an American was the USS Lewis Puller.

My name is Emma Susan Dodgson, and this is the small part I played in the rise of Jenna Plural.

CHAPTER ONE

—— ✳ ——

THE DAY IT ALL BEGAN

I took the bus from Arizona to Illinois. I know it was silly. No one takes buses these days other than tourists, and it even costs more than a plane due to the lack of demand. However, I had never left Sedona before. Well, unless you include trips into Phoenix and the surrounding area. Which I don't.

It was a good chance to see America before I left it. For the most part, I enjoyed it; however, staying in the seedy motels was most disconcerting when we stopped overnight. I headed out to buy cleaning supplies and bedsheets within minutes of seeing my room. I spent several hours cleaning it and changing the laundry before getting into my pajamas and going to bed. What made it even worse was that I'm sure the couple in the room next to me were either having physical relations or some vivid dreams. When I said my prayers that night, I mentioned them to my Lord.

I only slept a few hours and almost missed the bus leaving the next morning. I missed breakfast, which always made me cranky, so instead of reading my Bible as I had most of the journey, I curled up against the window and went to sleep. I slept several hours and was quite annoyed, having paid all this money and yet missing half of the greatest country that ever existed.

As we moved further north, the weather turned bleak, and it was not so fun anymore. I didn't want to look out of the dreary sky and gloomy streets. When we finally rolled into Chicago, it was even worse. It is a nasty little town that appeared only to invest money in its tall and ugly skyscrapers. Fortunately, I wasn't going to be staying there and made myself look out across Lake Michigan on the other side of the bus. We eventually reached our terminus, and my fellow passengers and I wearily traipsed off of the vehicle. I thanked the driver, but he only responded with a grunt. I can only assume he was very tired.

It was several more miles to get to The United States Marine training ground, where I was to begin my eleven weeks of basic training. I knew it was going to be tough. As I have told you, I made three attempts to join and barely passed when I finally did. I knew it would be grueling, but I knew I would make it with the Lord at my side.

I got a cab the rest of the way. A modern one that traveled much faster than the old-fashioned bus. It was less than ten minutes, and I was standing outside the front gates with my bag over my shoulder and excitement in my heart.

I walked to the guardpost where two marines were chatting, not noticing my approach. "Excuse me, Sir," I said nervously, my stammer more obvious than usual. The marine looked up at me. "I'm a new marine here to start my basic training." It startled me how fast he moved out of the cabin. He strode right up to me and put his face into mine so close that I stepped back, but he just stepped forward.

"Stand still." I complied. "You, miss, are not a marine," he screamed into my face. "You are nothing. You have to earn the right to call yourself a United States Marine. Have you earned that right?"

"No, Sir," I replied weakly.

This seemed to infuriate him even more. He pointed to the Gunnery Sergeant emblem on his sleeve. "Do I look like an officer, miss?"

"No, Sir." The moment I said it, I realized my mistake.

"Are you deaf? Do you need me to get you a hearing aid?" He bellowed.

"No, Sir." Holy heck, what was wrong with me? The problem was I was raised to call everyone I didn't know Sir or Ma'am.

His face was so close that I felt his spittle as he screamed at me. I could not help but blink. "Are you mental'y challenged? Do we need to put you down? Are we having learning difficulties?" he pointed down the pathway toward the main building, where I saw many marines parading up and down in various stages of their training. There was also a small group of people standing in civilian clothes. "That is where you are supposed to be. I made to move in that direction, but he stepped in front of me. "Did I say you could move?"

"No s... Gunnery Sergeant."

"What is your name?"

"Emma Dodgson"

"That is Emma Dobson, Gunnery Sergeant." The last two words were positively shrill.

"Emma Dodgson, Gunnery Sergeant."

He reached his hand out toward the other marine who had come up to join us while we were conversing. The man of a lower rank, which I cannot recall, handed him a tablet. He ran a finger down it, and I assume he checked my name off. He handed it back to the other man and stood upright with his hands by his sides. "Get moving, Dobson." I wanted to correct his use of my name but thought better of it, and I turned and started walking toward the main building. However, I found him walking along just behind me. "Pick those feet up, Dobson." I walked faster, "Run, Dobson." I started to run, but I guess it wasn't good enough as he screamed, "faster, Dobson." And I realized he was running behind me.

As we reached the group who were attempting to stand at attention, he screamed at me one last time. "Throw your pack down over there and fall into line." He pointed to where an array of bags were piled up, and I moved swiftly and dropped it amongst them, and then I joined the end of the line next to a tall gaunt man. The Gunnery Sergeant went over to another Sergeant and talked to him quietly. The other man looked up at me, and a deep scowl crossed his face. "Is there something over here that interests you, recruit?" he shouted.

"No, Sir," again, I knew I had made a fool of myself and turned my head to face front. I understand there was once a time when recruits called their drill instructors, Sir, And maybe if they still kept that going, things would have gone a lot differently for me.

I won't repeat it, but it was just as earlier. Did he look like an officer blah blah blah? He then admonished me for my crime, which had drawn his attention. "Your eyes will stay faced front, and you will not move them or yourself until you are told to. Am I clear?"

"Yes, Sergeant"

"Louder."

"Yes, Sergeant." With that, he moved away, and I felt a sense of relief as I stopped being the center of attention. We were not allowed to speak and remained standing until they unceremoniously led us into the quartermaster's to get our gear. It was like a production line. The person behind the counter would shout out, asking for your size, and you got a shirts, pants, boots, and so on. We were then let out into another room. We were made to line up along a white line. Just standing there holding our kit in our arms. Then he gave us the order to change. I hesitated. While there were several other women, it was mostly men and even those giving the orders were men. As the others were rapidly stripping off their clothes, the Sergeant saw me staring uncomfortably at them. He marched over to me, and with what would be normal for my next eleven weeks, he got into my face. "Did you hear my order?

"Yes, Sergeant."

"Do you know how to put on a uniform?"

"Yes, Sergeant."

"So, why aren't you doing it?"

13

I glanced down the line at the now naked bodies around me. I felt sick. When I gave my answer, I already knew that it would not be acceptable, and I found I could not deliver a coherent sentence and just said, "men, Sergeant."

"Oh dear, are we shy?" he shouted into my face, "The United States Marine Corps is an equal equity organization. We don't care if you are male or female, gay or straight, black or white, or green and blue. You will get changed now, or I'll ask some of these *men* to help you do it. Are we clear?"

I nodded and said, "yes, Sergeant." As I removed my clothing, I tried to fight back a tear. I believe I succeeded because had it been seen, I am sure the drill sergeant's wrath would have been down upon me again. I kept my eyes closed as I changed, only to open them when I absolutely had to. I didn't want to see the others looking at me. However, as I pulled off my shirt, I heard a man beside me. "What the fuck!"

I opened my eyes and looked at him in almost a panic. I assumed that he was looking at my breasts but realized instead that he was looking at the scars on my back. I hastily pulled on my uniform shirt and turned away from him.

Because of my delay, I was the last to finish, and of course, that drew more screams and shouts at me. I endured them.

Eventually, we were led to another room, where we were made to line up in a queue outside a door. Three at a time, recruits were sent in, and I heard the buzz, and I dreaded it. United States Marines were allowed to grow their hair long and have it tied up, but not in basic training. My long brown hair that had taken me years to grow down my back was about to depart. When my turn came, I entered. There were three barber seats, and as we went in, three recruits jumped up with newly shaved heads, and we took their places. I wanted to cry again as my long hair fell from my head. I started to wonder if I had bitten off more than I could chew. But no, the Lord wanted me here. He wanted me ready to fight the enemies of America. Whatever heck I was going to go through, it was my destiny to serve as a United States Marine.

My head felt cold as we ran from the barbers to the next room, where we were issued our rifles. We were then taken on to where we were to be billeted. There were no assigned bunks. We just took the one where we stopped in line as we ran to the end of the room. I was about halfway down, and I took the opportunity to glance around, hoping that those on either side of me would be female. One was, and the other wasn't, and I looked at him suspiciously. We stood at the end of the beds as the drill Sergeant walked down in front of us. He went through what would happen during this first week and told us to prepare our kits for inspection.

As the Sergeant left us alone, there was a collective sigh of relief, and the small buzz of conversation started.

"Hey there." I turned to see a short dark girl with a nice smile and perky cheeks. "I'm Lydia."

"Emma," I replied. "Nice to meet you. We started sorting out our kit, and I wondered what had happened to my belongings. I was not to see them again until the end of training.

"Nice to meet you, too, Emma. I'm from El Paso. Where are you from?"

"She's from dumb ass." A man, who I would come to know as Randall, said from the bunk opposite. He was not a very cultured man. Of course, I did not know him then, and I stared at him incredulously at his comment as he folded up a pair of pants.

"Is it really necessary for you to be vulgar, sir.?" I said, causing both him and several others within hearing to laugh.

"Oh my God, can you hear her?" he blasphemed. "I hear there's always one dumb ass in every boot camp. I think we have found ours." There were more laughs at my expense.

"Leave her alone," Lydia chided gently. "We are all in this together."

"That's total bullshit," he said sneeringly. "There are always those that shouldn't have got passed selection that holds the others back. She couldn't even get onto the campground without causing problems. She is going to be responsible for bringing down the team."

"That's not really fair. You haven't even given me a chance yet," I said, hoping that I would be able to reason with him, but he just sneered at me.

"Just do yourself and us a favor and quit before you drag us all down with you."

I could not help but blush and looked away dejectedly as I finished unpacking my kit. Had it not been for him distracting me, I probably wouldn't have made such a mess of it and, ten minutes later, got another bawling out in front of everybody. Again, doubts started to slip into my head, but the Lord was in my heart, and he calmed me. However, I already knew Randall Alice would be a problem that needed dealing with, and I was always good at dealing with problems like him.

CHAPTER TWO

— ❦ —

THE BULLY

"Come on, Emma, you can do it." As I lay in the mud, barely able to move, I did not believe Lydia's words of encouragement. "Move before the Sergeant sees you," she said when I still did not respond. My body ached, and I was tired of all the poop that was going on in this new life. We were only three weeks into this, and the thought of eight more was more excruciating than the pain that wracked my body. The wet mud was sucking me down, making it virtually impossible to shimmy along with my elbows as I was supposed to. I put in a final effort deciding that I would give up if this did not succeed. The suction beneath me made it all the harder to lift my body, but I made it. I moved out from under the barbed wire and started to get up on all fours to stand up. A boot came down on my neck, pushed my face back into the wet mud, and left me almost as soon as it came. I managed to lift my head slightly and saw the back of Randall as he raced on, having overtaken me. Lydia shouted some expletives after him, and I climbed up to my knees and asked her to cease

19

the vulgarity. She just stared at me. "Fuck you, Dodgson. I hung back to help you at the cost of my own time count. I've tried to be your friend, but you don't make it easy."

With that, she raced ahead and jumped up the climbing wall behind Randall. Then the voice we all feared came from behind me. "Get on your feet, Dobson." The Sergeant screamed, "What do you think this is? Naptime?"

I scrambled up as best I could. I looked back to where the Sergeant had come from. I knew that there was no way he did not see what Randall had just done to me. I had no time to ponder it more as he chased me up to the wall. Fortunately, I managed to clear it without much of a struggle. It was not just Randall who had made himself my enemy, but also the Sergeant.

That night I prayed to God to give me the strength to get through this and guide me on what I would do about the drill Sergeant and the demonic Randall. He gave me my answer, and I felt reassured as I went to sleep that night.

This intimidation continued until the fifth week when the final insult happened. Our furlough had been canceled because I had failed to complete a course in the allotted time, and they applied the 'if one fails, all fail' rule. The abuse was full on that night. I was called names that do not bear repeating. I just sat on my bed and took it. However, the furlough was reinstated the next day, and we all got ready to go out for the night. We were not allowed to leave until our uniforms were clean and pristine. I had made sure mine was perfect. I wanted to get away from this place for that night, not with the others but just out on my own.

I was in the bathroom when it happened. I was checking that I looked respectable in the mirror when someone came in and grabbed me from behind. I just managed to see in the reflection that it was Randall before he spun me around and pushed me into a toilet stall. I tried to put my training into action, but he quickly countered my move. Holding my arm behind my back, he pushed my head down into the toilet, which he had not flushed, but I'm not about to describe what was in there. He placed his knee upon my back and held me down as he flushed the toilet and the water swirled and splattered into my face and onto my clothing. "Give it up, Rapunzel, or this just gets worse." He released me and left. I fell to the floor and lay there spitting water. I climbed onto my knees and threw up violently into the bowl several times. I turned around on the floor, shut the door with my feet, and hugged my knees to my chin, sobbing softly.

I stayed there until everyone left. Nobody waited for me, not even Lydia, who had given up on her attempts to be friends with me. I didn't know what I had done wrong. I didn't care. When silence fell in the billet, I got up and took a long shower, scrubbing my face until it was red raw. I then got a fresh uniform, or rather the one I'd been wearing that day. It was certainly cleaner than the one I had prepared for the night out. I collected some things that I needed and headed out into the night.

I headed to the NCO's mess and ensured no one was watching me. I found the drill sergeant's Jeep, climbed into the back, and lay on the floor patiently. All the time, I prayed to God to grant me the patience and strength to

21

do what he wanted of me. I had been chosen to become a marine and kill America's enemies through divine decree. By default, the Sergeant was an enemy of America in trying to make me fail.

It was not as if I had a plan. I was letting the Holy Spirit guide me. I did not know how long I'd have to wait or even where the Sergeant would go when he came out. It felt ludicrous, expecting everything would fall in my favor. But that's the difference between people like me and people like you, who probably have little faith. Trust under God, and you cannot go wrong.

I lay there for almost two hours, not moving. I heard people coming and going and even talking right near the Jeep. But God kept the fear at bay, for he told me I would be safe.

Eventually, the Sergeant came out, and I recognized his voice even though the evil of liquor slurred it. His friend was trying to persuade him not to drive the Jeep, but he just laughed it off, climbed in, and started up the engine. As we started to move off, I took a gamble and looked out from underneath my blanket. I could see we were heading up the road toward the base's exit. We were not traveling fast, for he clearly liked being in control of his vehicle and did not switch on the automated systems that would drive itself.

We headed out to the streets, and I waited until we turned a few bends before I moved. You may think it's stupid that I made my move while traveling about forty miles an hour, but when you're armored by God, you are guaranteed safety.

My one disappointment was he never saw me, and he never knew who did it to him. However, I was not doing this for myself. I was doing this for my Lord and the American people. Wanting the credit for it is selfish, but I'm only human and flawed. I pulled out the length of wire I had taken from the base and curled the ends around my hands as I climbed up onto the seat behind him. He did not even look up in his mirror. I reached over his head and pulled it against his neck. He never even saw it coming. I pulled it tight, but I knew his physical strength would be greater than mine, so I twisted the ends around the back of the headrest.

I kept twisting as he clawed at his neck, and seconds later, we went off the road. I was thrown from the Jeep as it tipped onto its side, and I rolled down a small embankment on the side of the road. Apart from a couple of scrapes and bruises, I was unharmed, and I got up. I turned back to the Jeep, which was tipped up on its passenger side. He was still tied to the headrest and hung down to where his feet barely touched the ground. However, God was merciful, and it had been quick for him, for his neck snapped when the vehicle was turned over. I untied the wire, dropped it into the Jeep, and then reached down and opened the hood. It was a little bit of a struggle getting it to open, but I could reach in enough to wiggle the coolant wires until they came away. I then turned on the engine again, for it turned off automatically in the event of an accident. It hummed into life once more.

With my hands in my pockets, I started moving back to the base, humming 'America the Beautiful.' I was about halfway there when, behind me, the Jeep exploded. I looked back to see a tiny mushroom cloud go up into the night sky as the reactor overheated. I said a silent prayer thanking God for his guidance and asking for mercy upon the evil man's soul even though I knew there would be none.

God had no mercy for the enemies of the United States of America.

I slept well that night, and we even got an extra hour to lie in as the Sergeant failed to report for duty. Fortunately, a car reactor overheating doesn't leave much of the body for a decent autopsy, and in time it was concluded that he died in a drunk driving accident. Everyone was a little shocked at the death of our Sergeant, and the fact that we got the next few days off of training made everyone in my billet very happy. I wanted to tell them they had me to thank for it, but I doubt they would have believed me. The next two weeks went a lot smoother, even Randall laid off me, and I think that's because we got a new drill Sergeant to replace the heathen one. She was not much better than him but didn't directly attempt to fail me.

I enjoyed the hand-to-hand combat best, for I imagined looking into a Peon's face, and he would look into my eyes at the American who was about to dispatch him to heck. My body started to become accustomed to the vigorous torture, which I suppose was the point.

Graduation was coming fast, and I had to turn my attention to dealing with Randall. I realized I could not let him have the privilege of becoming a United States Marine. It would dishonor a proud legacy. However, the opportunity did not seem to come up. It was most frustrating. However, I did not allow myself to dwell on it as I knew the Lord would grant me an opportunity at some time.

Graduation day finally came, and thanks to God, I had made it. Barely. Parents began arriving, and I looked out eagerly to find mine. I had really hoped they would come. I wanted them to be proud of me, and I watched as mothers and fathers, brothers and sisters, gushed over their precious offspring in their dress uniforms. When the new marines had the opportunity to show their family around in a more relaxed atmosphere, I returned to my billet, sat on my bed, and read.

I was surprised when someone came in. I was not expecting anybody. But Randall came up to his bed opposite mine. I tried to ignore him, but there was new ammunition to fire at his cannon fodder. "Wow, Rapunzel, even your parents hate you, don't they?" He chuckled as he opened his locker to get something. Of course, I did not rise to his juvenile debate and simply ignored him. He looked down at my bible. "I really can't believe that you believe all that bullshit." Again I didn't answer. "Hey," he said, and this time he stepped around to my side of the bunk and leaned against it looking down at me. "If you're into all that shit, does that mean you're still a virgin?" I simply turned the page, but I wasn't actually reading now. "You know I could fix that for you." I slowly raised my eyes toward him and gave him a disgusted look. He just laughed. "Nah, just kidding. I would have to be pretty desperate to wanna fuck you. You'll probably get captured on your first mission and pop your cherry with a dozen sex-starved Peons. They don't care who they fuck."

"You are the most uncouth and vulgar man I have ever met, Private Alice. You are a disgrace to that uniform you wear." That was possibly the worst thing you could say to a marine; however, he was a demon in marine clothing, and he had pushed all my buttons.

His grinning face turned angry, and he stepped forward, raising the back of his hand to me. I did not move. I just sat there and smiled, knowing that that strike would end with him in the stockade. Unlike the toilet incident, he ran the risk of leaving a mark. He paused as he realized this and lowered his hand, sneering, "you are not worth it, Rapunzel." He turned away and headed to the bathroom. "See you in hell, bitch."

As the bathroom door shut behind him, I carefully closed my bible and gently laid it aside. I got up and opened the drawer beside my bunk. I lifted my cotton briefs and picked up the combat knife I kept for such an opportunity.

Gently humming, 'My Country Tis of Thee," I headed to the bathroom. I opened the door and stepped in. I looked under the gap beneath the doors of each cubicle until I found him. I felt a little guilty at the indignity of what was about to happen. His trousers around his ankles, sitting in the john would be a most undignified way to go out of this world.

Of course, the cubicle was locked, but it was not exactly designed to keep some criminal element out. I stepped away from it, took a quick step forward, and slammed my boot against the door. It flew open, and he sat, looking up at me, the epitome of startled. He scrambled to get to his pants.

I stepped up to him, placed a hand on his forehead, and slammed his head back against the cistern behind him. Before he could recover, I grabbed his hair and whacked his head back several times until he was too groggy to retaliate effectively. "Rapunzel." He was barely audible. I kept slamming his head until I was sure he was no threat

I stood with my legs on either side of his and held his head back. I smiled down at him as he stared up at me, trying to gather his senses. When he made to speak again, I just spat into his mouth. I did it slowly, watching my saliva travel down until it reached him. I feel bad about that. It was unnecessary, but I guess there is a dark side even to me.

I started to sing to him softly, like a mother comforting a child. "My country 'tis this wee sweet land of liberty." Holding his head back, I unfastened the golden buttons on his dress uniform and opened it. "Of thee I sing. Land where my fathers died." I pulled the knife from my belt. "Land of the pilgrim's pride." I felt down his rib cage to find the last one. "From every mountainside." I thrust it hard under his rib and straight up into his heart, just as I had been trained. "Let freedom ring." As I did, I folded his jacket over my hand to stop blood from coming over my uniform.

His eyes widened as he stared at me and tried to speak. "Hush," I said softly in my best motherly voice as I let go of the knife and raised a blood-spattered finger to my lips. "Don't try to say anything. Just go to sleep." He blinked, a tear ran down his eye, and he fell limply against the side of the cubicle. I calmly felt for the pulse in his neck, and as soon as I was sure he was dead, I stepped back. I did not remove the knife, which would surely have gotten more blood on me.

I pulled out my hanky and wiped the handle down. Sure, they would find my DNA on him, there was no doubt about that, but there were many exercises we had been performing over the last eleven weeks that we all would have come into physical contact with him. Yep, there would be my DNA and the DNA of twenty others. Even the knife could not be traced back to me as I had stolen it. Well, I shouldn't really say stolen, as stealing is wrong. I borrowed it and could not be blamed if the authorities did not return it to its owner. I did feel a pang of guilt for leaving him to be found in such an I'm dignified position. But then, he was a heathen blasphemer and was now suffering the ultimate indignities in heck.

I stepped out of the 'cubicle and washed my hands and face. Once more, humming 'My Country Tis of Thee,' I went back into the main barrack room and climbed out of the back window. I ensured I was seen around the parade ground by as many men, women, officers, and instructors as possible. It took about an hour before he was discovered, and of course, the base was immediately locked down.

In the following days, I was subject to boring interviews with military police, as was everyone. I was on the suspect list after the animosity between us was reported. But no one honestly believed that the skinny pale girl from Arizona could have taken out the six foot three muscle-bound bully. It did have the annoying effect of delaying us from being able to depart by another week.

They eventually allowed us to leave for a ten-day furlough before receiving our posts. This time I took the fifteen-minute flight home. I had written to my parents to tell them I was on my way, but I didn't expect anyone to pick me up from the airport.

I come from a very military family, with my father and most of my aunts and uncles having served. However, I was an embarrassment to my dad as they had all been commissioned officers, and I didn't make the grade for that. My dad was a strict disciplinarian and quick with the back of his hand or his belt. While the bible says to honor thy parents, he solely tested that rule with my brother and me. I had pondered not going home even as late as when I was in a cab taking me up into the mountains. But I did want to see Sedona one last time before being shipped out.

I received details of my first posting before I left. They were going to put me on the USS Lewis Puller, and I looked it up on the internet to find out it was named after the most decorated man in the marine corps. I could not find any details about the ship itself, so I was disappointed that it was apparently unimportant. It was also the first time I had heard her name. Although in its more proper form of Jenacia Plularian. You know her now as Admiral Jenna Plural of the Solar Confederation. She was just a Lieutenant back then and was to be my commanding officer. The post was to be for two years, and although it didn't say it, that clearly meant I was going off-world.

The car pulled up outside my house. I climbed out and grabbed my kit bag from the trunk. I walked up the pathway and opened the door, which my parents rarely locked despite my objections. I went inside. My brother grunted at me from the couch where he was playing video games. I dropped my kit bag in the hallway and went to the kitchen where my mother was cooking. "Oh, hi honey, did you have a nice time at boot camp," she said casually, glancing over her shoulder.

"Hello, mother. You make it sound like I just got back from a church summer camp," I said snappily.

She just sighed and turned back to her counter. "Your father's coming home early tonight. I really must get on with this."

I sighed and rolled my eyes, and headed up to my room. Picking up Mr. Hupperty, my stuffed pink hippopotamus, I curled up on the bed and hugged him tightly to my chest.

I went to sleep.

CHAPTER THREE

— ❋ —

GOODBYE SEDONA

"The USS Lewis Puller?" My dad said with obvious contempt, "I have never heard of the USS Lewis Puller. Who is Lewis Puller anyway?"

We were seated at the breakfast table. My dad, a retired naval veteran, had only just asked about my assignment despite my having been home for ten days. He was not very impressed, and he made it very clear.

I sat there, somewhat irritated. This was to be my first posting, and he was ruining it. "Lewis Puller was a Marine who was awarded more medals than anyone else in America."

"How do you know that?" He scoffed.

"I looked it up."

"Exactly. You don't name ships after people no one's heard of unless they're useless. You should be on that new USS Constitution."

"It's probably a garbage hauler." That was my kid brother Scott who sat opposite me. He was a mouthy little tyke still in high school.

31

"Finish your breakfast, Scotty," my mother called over from the kitchen counter. "The school bus is going to be here in ten minutes."

"Yeah yeah, I'm doing it," he muttered and looked down at his food.

I grinned at him patronizingly and felt a sharp kick under the table. I reciprocated with my boot, causing him to jump up, spilling the milk from his bowl. I had steel toecaps on, nice shiny new ones that went with my new uniform. "Fuck you, you bitch."

My dad turned red with rage and stood up. "Watch that mouth of yours, boy. I won't tolerate that language in this house. Apologize to your sister at once."

"She's in the United States Marines, Dad," Scott said incredulously, "Do you think they're gonna talk like powder puffs?"

My father moved so fast that I barely saw it, and he backhanded Scott violently. My brother staggered, but before my father could strike him again, I was up out of my seat, and I grabbed his wrist. He glared at me, his face reddening and the vein on his forehead throbbing. "Is this really how you want my last morning here to be," I shouted. "I am going out into space today and won't be back for at least two years. Can we, for once, finish something without this drama?"

Before he could reply, Scotty snatched up his bag, and he looked at me with sadness in his eyes. "Have a good war, sis." He strode out as I still held onto my father's wrist, and the last I saw of him was the back of the door as he slammed it closed behind him. My eyes turned to my father, and I let go of his arm. He instantly moved to slap me around the face, but the marines don't train you to let that slide. My arm swiftly blocked the strike. My mother moved between us. "You are an ungrateful brat Emma Dodgson." my father said.

"Maybe so, Dad, Maybe so." I looked at my mother. "I'm sorry about this."

My mother, fearing him for most of her life, did not even make eye contact with me. "Perhaps you should just go," she said.

I fought back the tears in my eyes, not knowing if they were out of sadness or anger. I turned away from the table, picked up my kit bag, and headed out the front door. It was to be the last time I ever spoke to my parents. Dad was an angry man, and he had always taken it out with his fists on the rest of us. I kind of both love him and hate him at the same time. He never accepted that I was enlisted and not an officer like him. Heck, my school grades barely qualified me to be enlisted, and no one was going to consider me for a commission. At least, that is what I thought back then. That was before Jenna Plural.

There was a cool breeze as I stepped out onto the streets of Sedona for the last time. I loved this old town up in the mountains of Arizona. I had attended the Sedona Red Rock High School, Home of the Scorpions, and had never really left the tourist town other than trips into Phoenix. I hope to go back there one day, but I digress...

I walked down the street and turned the corner. I looked out over the valley at the rust-covered mountains with a sigh. I dropped my kitbag and stayed out there for about fifteen minutes staring at the scenery, and then I tapped my watch. "This is Private Emma Dodgson 1313978 to Phoenix base requesting pick up."

There was a few seconds' pause before a voice came back. "We read you Private Dodgson 1313978. You are early. We are not scheduled to pick you up for another two hours."

"Yes, Sir. However, I'm ready, but I can kill time if that helps?" I replied.

"It would. I can't get anything out to you for at least an hour. "

"Affirmative, Sir. Do you wish to give me a location for pick up?"

"Activate your locator, Private. The transport will find you," he advised me.

"Thank you, Sir."

"No problem, Private, and good luck on the Lewis Puller."

I tapped the watch again to disconnect the communications, and then I voice-activated my locator, which sent out a GPS signal that only the US military could pick up. I picked up my bag again and walked into town, where I stopped at a small café. It was not very busy, and I ordered a coffee and a cooked breakfast.

I was lost in my thoughts as I ate, and I did not see Calvin Butler come in. "Hey, Em."

I looked up at my old high school boyfriend and half-smiled. This was awkward. I had only recently broken up with him because I was leaving. He was headed to university on a football scholarship, and our lives were on very different paths. "Hey, Cal."

He slipped into the seat opposite me, and as I looked at those big brown eyes, I felt my heart beating fast. The guy was such a honey. "I went to your house, and your parents said you had already left. I just wanted to say goodbye."

"How did you know I was here?"

"I didn't. I work in the hardware store next door, remember? I saw you as I was headed into work." He sat back.

"I'm sorry things didn't work out between us," I said.

Cal shrugged. "They still can. I care about you, and I know you still care about me. "

I sighed wearily, not wanting to do this all over again. "We have different lives now. You're going off to college, then become some corporate financier, and I will be fighting Peons around the rings of Saturn."

Cal sighed. "You wanna fight? That's fine, but why not do it here? You know the war is headed this way. Texas has already fallen, and there's fighting already going on east of here. You don't need to leave."

"Even if I didn't have to leave. It's all done and dusted now. It's not like I could tell the US Marine Corps, 'hey, I wanna stay at home.' They tell me where to go, when to eat, and when to sleep."

Calvin gave a sigh of resignation, but he didn't give up, "I saw a future for us. We get married, get a little house and a couple of kids. Boys who grow up to be little jocks." he smiled, but I did not return it.

"Hey, I didn't get a scholarship and the grades for college. Military service was always going to be compulsory for me."

35

"Yeah, but military service is just for two years. You signed up to the marines as a non-conscript regular. The minimum requirement is six years."

"As a conscript, I'd be army infantry, virtually cannon fodder. At least this way, I'll have some sort of career out of it."

"That's more important than us?"

"Cal," I said sharply. "Stop trying to make this even harder. You know my situation at home. I always told you that I would get out at the first opportunity. Anyway, I'm proud to be a marine, and I'm going to make a career of it. You're going to find a nice girl and settle down in your house with your two boys." Before he could say anymore, my communicator buzzed. "Private Dodgson, go ahead." My eyes were still on Calvin, but they quickly dropped to my wrist communicator as I heard an Australian woman singing. "Pack up your troubles in your old kit bag and smile, smile, smile."

"Excuse me?"

"G'day, Private Dobson, this is Stacey Airlines. I will be your pilot for your one-way trip to hell."

I looked up at Calvin with wide eyes, and he looked as bemused as me. "Excuse me, ma'am, can you clarify that?" I asked.

"I'm your ride to Manassas, you moron." The voice came back. "Lieutenant Stacey Grant of the United States Navy. I'm about to put down at your location."

"Ma'am, this is a downtown high street. You really can't land a shuttle here. Let me know where I can move to, and I will meet you there."

"This ain't no shuttle, Private. I'm in a Python interceptor."

"They sent a fighter to pick me up, ma'am?"

"Don't you watch the news, Dobson? Arizona is a designated war zone. You have Peons less than fifty miles from this location. Uncle Sam doesn't want his nice, new recruit to start her career as a big mass of bullet-ridden jelly."

It was only then that I could hear the roar of the engines. Dust started to blow up from the road covering the surrounding parked cars, and everybody started to come out of the shop doorways down the street. Then the sleek black craft descended out of the clouds and landed slap bang in the middle of the road. Calvin looked at it and then back at me. "I guess that's my ride," I said to him softly.

He came out with me, carrying my kit bag, and I felt the eyes of the entire street upon me. The cockpit of the Python Interceptor opened up, and the pilot looked down at me as the engines died. "G'day mate. Private Emma Dobson?"

I gave her a sharp salute, and she half-heartedly returned it. "It is Dodgson, Ma'am."

"What?"

"My name. It is Dodgson, not Dobson."

"Yeah, well, unless you need to give your boyfriend a blowjob to keep him sweet, we gotta get moving."

I flushed bright pink, and any chance of a romantic goodbye with Calvin was gone.

I grabbed my kit bag from him and simply said, "I'll see you around sometime." Then I climbed onto the wing, stowed my kit bag behind the empty seat, and climbed into it. As the canopy closed, I looked down at Calvin, but he was already walking away. I placed the headphones on to hear the pilot and sat back in the seat, fastening my seat belt.

The pilot called control to radio in her flight plan. We certainly did not want to be shot down as an enemy air-craft. "This is Lieutenant Stacey Grant lifting off from Sedona. Transmitting navigation routes. I will be flying around the front lines. ETA in Manassas, in just over twelve minutes."

"That's a copy, Lieutenant Grant. Clear skies to you," came the flight control reply. I looked once more for Calvin and saw him standing on the corner of the street where he had turned round to watch. I gave him a wave, but he did not reciprocate, so I let my hand fall onto my lap and looked away as the craft rose vertically up into the sky.

I decided this pilot was a little bit crazy as she pulled up before the DE compensators came online, and I was pushed violently back into my seat.

Everything became virtually a blur to me. I could barely understand how this Stacey Grant could even follow what was happening. However, I did not have time to think about it. Within seconds Grant threw the craft into a roll. "Shit, those mother fuckers pushed forward the frontline further than we thought." To be in the company of Stacey Grant, one had to get used to her rather salty language. "We have three Dutch Viper class fighters coming up after us."

"Can we lose them, ma'am?"

"Lose them." Lieutenant Grant laughed, "No, Private Dobson, we blow those fuckers out of the sky."

"If you say so, ma'am," I said nervously.

"Hey, trust me, I'm Australian." she giggled like a twelve-year-old schoolgirl as we suddenly flipped down and began to spiral.

I looked out of the canopy windows and felt momentary nausea as the world spun about me. She then straightened up and shot straight back up into the air. I was startled to see an enemy aircraft appear to drop down in front of us. We were mere feet away from it as Grant fired the primary weapons. There was a hiss, and then a bang as the rear of the enemy aircraft erupted into flame and began to spin out of control, plummeting to the Earth. "That's one of the tulip fuckers." The foul-mouthed Aussie punched the roof of the canopy in celebration. We again fell into a spin as I saw her evade a couple of missiles on our left. "I hope you haven't pissed your pants back there, Private." She laughed.

"I am doing quite fine, ma'am," I said, just as Grant spun us in a one-eighty turn and fired straight into the front of another craft. We shook slightly as shrapnel from the exploding vessel hit us, but this pilot was darn good. The final pilot started working out her tactics and got on our tail, and he or she did not move from that position. Our craft bumped up and down in random directions as missile after missile came at our rear. Grant's sudden silence made me uneasy as I realized we were in trouble. Then suddenly, she pushed her craft into a dive and headed straight to the ground at an unbelievable speed. The darn Peon on our tail stayed on us, copying the dive and still firing. Stacey pulled up sharply at what seemed like inches from the ground, and the engines whined in protest. If she had intended for him to hit the ground before pulling up, she failed, and he stuck with us. However, as he was pulling up, she released a ton of flack straight down upon his canopy. I did not see what happened, but I heard the craft explode as we were already shooting off across the US and out of the contested airspace.

CHAPTER FOUR

ABOARD THE CHESTY

We landed just outside the cosmodrome in a small field of other interceptors. Grant waited until I climbed out and followed me as naval personnel rushed around doing postflight checks. "Welcome home, ma'am." a young, heavily built marine sergeant walked up to us with a beaming smile, but the smile was not to last long.

"Wow," Stacey said somewhat irritably, "I must be way off course then."

"Ma'am?" the sergeant frowned.

"This must be Wagga."

"I am not sure I understand, ma'am."

"You said welcome home. My home is in Australia, mate."

"Yes, ma'am, no offense intended, ma'am."

"None was taken, Sergeant Hardy. Carry on." She stepped past him and headed off toward the astrodrome. Hardy muttered something about her being a bitch and turned his wrath upon me. "What are you staring at, Private?"

"Nothing Sir." I stood at attention, immediately realizing my mistake, but it was too late.

"Sir? Do I look like an officer, Dobson?" he spat.

"No, Sergeant."

"That's better, rookie. Now get your lazy ass over there." He indicated where another group of privates stood nervously near the entrance of the cosmodrome, and I saw Grant giving them a cheery wave as she passed them. I put my kit over my shoulder and started to walk over to them, but Hardy shouted, "double time Private Dodgson." I broke into a run and reached the group thirty seconds later. There were five of them. I don't remember their names, but the one that cannot go without mentioning was Kelsey Anthony. She was the closest thing I had to a friend in those first days. Sadly it was not to last. She smiled at me as I approached, being the only other female in the group. "Thank God there's another woman around." These were her first words to me. "This testosterone around me was getting somewhat tiresome."

One of the men grinned at us. "You should enjoy the opportunity, Anthony. I hear there are not many men on this ship." I think his name was Berkeley, but I am not sure. Let's just go with Berkeley.

"Fuck you, Berkeley, not even if you were the last man on Earth."

He puffed up his chest in a vain effort to look sexy. "Well, that's fine because we're not gonna be on Earth in a few hours, and I'll be all yours baby."

"And that gets you two hundred push-ups, marine," Hardy said, coming up behind us. Berkeley looked like he was going to argue. "Four hundred. Hit the dirt, mister."

Berkley complied, and I smiled at the sergeant but not for long. "If you don't want to join him, Dobson, take that stupid grin off your face." Turning back to Berkeley, he said, "if I catch you sexually harassing female troopers again, you will spend the rest of this voyage in the M.E.T. without pay and face a court-martial on your return." No one spoke; the only sound was the huffing and puffing of Berkeley as he did his push-ups. Hardy turned around to each marine in turn. "Is this the best they can give me? I guess that's what happens when you're on a shit stain of a ship." Hardy sighed with resignation. "Well, don't just stand there. Get moving at the double." We broke into a run and went through the astrodome's large rusty doors and into the wreck of a base.

It was just as Mr. Phelker described in his book. Dilapidated with signs of bombing damage. The U.S.S. Lewis Puller was just like he said as well. A heaving wreck of a vessel that was badly patched.

"Everybody halt," Hardy ordered. We all complied and stood at attention. "Everyone line up in front of the cargo bay ramp." Again, we complied with the five of us facing out from the clapped-out vessel. We stood in an at-ease position. Hardy was about to speak but then appeared to notice something behind us. "Attention," he shouted. "Officer on the deck."

At first, I was confused as some coed in an officer's uniform stepped out in front of us. She bore lieutenant chevrons and was undoubtedly one of the most beautiful women I had ever seen. She had long light brown hair tied very neatly into a tail and blue eyes that seemed to sparkle. "The new recruits, ma'am," Hardy informed her.

"Good morning, boys and girls. My name is Jenna Plural, and I'm the Second Officer on board the U.S.S. Lewis Puller. I know you're probably itching to get your hands on the enemy, but unfortunately, it won't be on this trip. Your duties will be in support. And I regret to inform you that, for most of this mission, you will be uploaded in the M.E.T. for most of the voyage. You will only be downloaded if we are attacked en route to our destination or other unforeseen circumstances arise. When we are ready to launch, you will be uploaded and most likely not downloaded again until we return to Earth. I apologize that you will not get much experience on this voyage, but you will get full credit for your service. Until you are uploaded, you can use the crew cabins as your more experienced crewmates are already uploaded. However, you will have pre-launch ship preparation duties that Sergeant Hardy will hand out to you. You have one hour to get yourself ready and stow your kit. Dismissed." She turned away and spoke to Hardy.

Kelsey turned to me. "Come on, let's go find a cabin before the guys take the best ones. "

I grinned and followed her inside, eager to find a cabin where I could shower and change. We grabbed the first one we saw. It was a four-man berth, but we had it to ourselves. There was no gender segregation in the military, but I was happy not to share with men. "So, where are you from?

I told her as I unpacked my kitbag and asked her in return. "I'm from Chicago and grew up there. This is my first time away from home for basic training," she told me.

"Same here. My father was military, but we never moved with him." As I pulled out a change of uniform from my kitbag, my small black Bible fell out and landed on the floor. I thought nothing of it. As I picked it up, Kelsey looked at me with surprise. "You're a Christian?"

As I stuffed the Bible back into the bag, I looked at her with a raised eyebrow, "Is that a problem?" I said irritably.

She raised her hands, indicating no offense. "No, it's just unusual. You rarely meet one of these days."

I shrugged that off. "Not where I come from. Sedona has become a haven for the evangelical church. Nearly everyone in town is a member. "

A cheeky look crossed her face as she asked, "if you're practicing a Christian doesn't that mean you're... a ... umm."

She did not finish her sentence yet waited for me to reply, but I honestly had no clue what she meant, "I'm a what?? "

"Well, have you never been with a man or a woman?"

I think I turned red and spat back, "That's kind of a personal question, don't you think?"

She shrugged, but she also grinned as if she knew the answer. If she thought such an idea embarrassed me, it was far from the truth. My virtue was my affair, and suggesting that I could have been with a woman was utterly disgusting.

"You don't know what you're missing out on." She smirked.

"Oh, I certainly do," I said, referring to my spiritual salvation. She looked a little confused, but I changed the subject, and she went with it.

We both took turns showering, and I put on a fresh uniform, and together we both reported for duty.

As you already know, the U.S.S. Lewis Puller, affectionately known as The Chesty, was a small, dark, dreary ship. As Kelsey and I explored, our excitement turned to grim depression. This was to be our home for two years, and its only redeeming quality was that we would spend most of it in the nothingness of the M.E.T.

We met a woman dressed in civvies when we got down to the engine area. She wore immodestly tight jeans over an equally tight hoodie and spoke with a thick New York accent. She smiled as she came up to us. "Hey, nice to see some fresh faces." I was unsure how to address her at first, for she bore no indication of her rank, so I left it to Kelsey to say, "nice to meet you, ma'am."

The redheaded woman grinned, "I'm not a ma'am. But obviously, you can't tell that while I'm off duty. Gunnery Sergeant Helen Tracker. I'm chief tech of this vintage pride of the fleet."

Kelsey chuckled. "Vintage? Nice way to put it, sergeant."

Helen returned the grin, "well, don't let Lieutenant Plural hear you diss the U.S.S. Lewis Puller. She'll put you on report."

"She likes this ship?" I asked wide-eyed.

"Oh, she knows it's a heap of junk like the rest of us."
Tracker laughed. "But she believes you should take pride
in any ship you serve aboard. This ship should have been
retired many years ago. However, since we lost our last
construction base on Mars, we must make do and mend."

"We are losing this war, aren't we?" Kelsey said, much to
my horror.

"Don't ever say that," I said curtly. "America has not lost
a war in hundreds of years, and it's not about to now. I
think it should be treason even to suggest such a thing."
There was silence as both Tracker and Kelsey stared at me.

"Umm, yes, well, there is a welcome party in the mess,"
Tracker said. "Come by in about thirty minutes, and we'll
have a proper marine welcome for you."

I said nothing, for my blood was still boiling, but Kelsey
smiled and said, "Now that sounds like a plan."

Tracker smiled at her, glanced awkwardly at me, and
walked off. We continued our tour of the ship, famil-
iarizing ourselves with its layout and emergency procedures until it was time to go to the mess. It was small and
cramped like most of the ship, and about a half dozen
marines and a couple of naval personnel were already
knocking back cold beers. It was a mixture of new and a
couple of veteran crewmen, and Berkeley was there trying
to hit on some woman who was obviously uninterested.
The guy was a creep, and there was no mistaking that. It
was a long time since the military tolerated such acts, but
it still didn't stop them from happening. Sexual impropriety was your one-way ticket out of the military and into
prison. I could see that Berkeley was in for a short career. I

pondered dealing with him myself, but he was dead three weeks later anyway.

A Lance Corporal, who I later found out was called Neuman, was frying up eggs, bacon, and sausages. When the marines scoffed them down, he protested. "You have to save some for the officers."

"You can make them some ham sandwiches," laughed another marine.

Someone threw us both cans of Budweiser, which we cracked open. "I was waiting for you to say you don't drink," giggled Kelsey at my expense.

"I'm not a Mormon, you know," I replied rather irritably.

"Sheeze, Emma, don't you have a sense of humor?"

"Of course, but only when someone says something that is actually funny."

I did not realize this would be overheard. It raised a laugh from many of my colleagues around me. "Hey guys," Helen Tracker stepped into the room, grinning. "It plays merry hell with your system if you go through the M.E.T. intoxicated." She had changed into the marine uniform but wore the pink hoodie over it. I could not help but think how inappropriate that was.

Now I know what you are thinking. I was some kind of prudish stuck-up little know-it-all who played by the book. The truth is I was back then but stick with me. Very soon, all of that was going to change.

Kelsey seemed to fit right in and was proving to be quite popular, while I was more a fifth wheel standing silently beside her. A pleasant time was had by most until the sergeant came in and brought it to an end.

Hardy was his usual unpleasant self, but he put Berkeley on bathroom duties which pleased both Kelsey and me, so we didn't really complain when he had us inventorying the cargo supplies in the hold. It was a laborious mind-numbing task. However, we were interrupted when Lieutenant Plural, in a rather indecently small tank top and shorts, came running down the deck with Stacey Grant close behind her. "Their shuttle has just disappeared off the radar." Lieutenant Plural was telling the young Australian. "It must have come down somewhere near Virginia Beach."

"I could take out an interceptor. It will be much faster." Grant suggested.

"Too fast. If they bailed out, you'd hardly spot an individual."

"Good point, boss. We can send up a drone. It can fly in low and has a fairly good range before it needs refueling." As they passed us, we stood to attention and saluted. Lieutenant Plural gave a brief, half-hearted salute back, and oh so unprofessionally, Grant gave me a wink.

"Go for it, and while you're doing that, I will see if I can get satellite coverage of the area," Lieutenant Plural said as the two went on to the main hub of the base.

Kelsey and I looked at each other, wondering what was going on, but we just continued with our work. Fifteen minutes later we saw a drone going up into the air from the other side of the astrodome's wall. We listened to the hum of the engine until it disappeared from our view and then simply carried on checking off the boxes. About thirty minutes later, Lieutenant Plural came running out of the hub. She headed over to where cars were parked on the outer circle of the astrodome and jumped into one. Seconds later, she tore out of the base.

When we were finishing up, the car with Mr. Phelkar and Lieutenant Plural pulled back into the astrodrome. We both watched as he got out. He was staring at the Lewis Puller, looking horrified at the vessel. "Well, isn't he a cutie," Kelsey said with a grin. "I'd love to wrap my legs around that face."

"Plus, he has that adorable English accent that you young American girls love so much." I turned to see Grant grinning at us.

Kelsey flushed pink and stood to attention. "Yes, ma'am."

"What about you, Dobson? Wouldn't you like a piece of that arse?"

It was my turn to flush, and I just blustered incoherently, which caused Grant to grin. "At ease, ladies. Don't bust a blood vessel, Dobson. "

"It's Dodgson, ma'am."

"Yeah yeah, whatever," she muttered but was already stepping past us and walking up to Mr. Phelkar. "She ain't as bad as she looks," she said to him.

He turned to face her. "Lieutenant Grant, I presume?" he said as Lieutenant Plural turned toward me and beckoned me over.

"Got it in one, mate," Grant was saying.

Lieutenant Plural handed me his bag and said, "stow it aboard the ship," and then sent Kelsey to drive the car away as I headed up the ramp back into the ship.

That bum-hole Hardy was waiting for me in the doorway. "Have you finished that inventory?"

"Yes, Sergeant, the Lieutenant asked me to put away this bag for the civilian visitor."

"Then move yourself, Dobson. And then get to the M .E.T. it's time for upload."

I sighed. Would anyone ever get my name right? Hardy looked down the ramp to where Mr. Phelkar and Lieutenant Grant were coming up. He said nothing more to me, so I hurried past, wondering where the heck I was to put this bag and wondering why it was so freaking dirty. In the end, I just stored it in my cabin, which I guess was as good as any place. Then headed over to get uploaded. I had only been a M.E.T once before. They gave us that experience back in basic training, so it would not come as a surprise to us. The one thing I would always be uncomfortable with, was removing our clothes, storing them in cabin lockers, and then heading down the corridor to the M.E.T. room. But that was life in the modern USMC. We double-timed it to get there before any of the guys did. And fortunately, we made it. I went in first. I met Helen Tracker, and there were no preliminaries. Tracker barked the orders. "Stand in the circle." I complied. "Raise your arms. " I complied again, and there was a flash of light this time. As the glow faded, I looked back at Tracker, wondering just for a moment if it had gone wrong. "We are under attack. Move out and get kitted up." She instructed.

DAVID PARKER-ROSS

It was not until much later I realized that three weeks had passed and we were only halfway to our Mars destination.

CHAPTER FIVE

— ❖ —

BOARDED

I headed out into the corridor. Two other marines had come out ahead of me, and already another came out behind me. "Faster, Dobson. You're not walking down the aisle at your wedding." Sergeant Hardy barked.

I followed the others down to the portside corridor and found a uniform waiting for me on the floor with chest armor and a snap pistol. I dressed quickly as I was trained to. Kelsey came to my side, looking much more nervous than I felt. We helped fasten each other's armor, and there was a buzz of conversation as we all tried to work out what was going on.

It fell silent when Lieutenant Plural stood at the end of the corridor. We came to attention. She waited until all fell silent, standing with legs apart and hands behind her back. We felt the tension grow, and the only sound was the soft hum of the engine.

She swung out a fist and hit the intercom. "Froggy comes, a calling." She paused., "they want to take your ship," she paused again. "but just like the man this ship is named after, we shall give them no quarter." Another pause. "we shall make them pay in Peon blood for every square foot of our ship," her voice rose as she spoke. "They're coming from the port side, and we will expect full hull penetration. We will not let these Peon bastards win the day." Then she screamed out, "We are United States Marines. What are we?"

"United States Marines," We replied in unison, and it echoed around the ship.

"Fall in on the port corridor and prepare for battle." She raised her fist and pumped in the air three times, chanting, "U.S.A. U.S.A. U.S.A." In unison, we stamped our right foot on the floor in the unofficial salute of our commanding officer. Then, we ran to our positions and turned to face the wall with weapons raised to our hips.

An eerie silence fell all around us, and only the slight hum of the engines and vibrations of the decks could be heard. We waited. There was a boom, and it rang through the deck in an aftershock. The line of Marines tensed. "Easy boys and girls, just gonna be like squishing frog spawn," Lieutenant Plural called down the line. "Pascal, stop scratching your ass, and Butterwick, hold up that ugly head of yours. You are killing Peons, not going down on your boyfriend." The others laughed at this. I didn't get what it meant.

I felt very tense as the drilling started. I knew what was coming. We had undergone intensive and repetitive training on repelling borders but didn't prepare you for that feeling in your gut knowing that, in a few moments, it was killer be killed. Next to us, the bulkhead suddenly disintegrated before our eyes, and the two marines in front of it fired into the dark. I saw the body of a man in the light blue uniform of the French fall through the hole, and suddenly the Marine next to me flew back against the wall, his face a bloodied pulp.

When the hole opened up in front of me, I was face to face with a large angry looking woman, and I fired. As she went down, I felt the thrill of dispensing God's justice, and I found myself laughing as I continued to fire at the Peon scum.

I saw Kelsey go down in my peripheral vision, but I could do nothing but hold the line. Then I heard Lieutenant Plural cry out, "grenade." Hastily I stumbled down the corridor and over the bodies of comrades and Peons, following my teammates out of the corridor and away from the expected explosion. It turned out to be just a pesky flashbang. When we reached the larger hallway, a couple of us turned back and fired down the corridor. Berkeley suddenly went down at my side with a hole in his head just above his right eye. I was convinced I would die that day, but I was going to make sure I took out as many of those darn Peons as I could.

Like a swarming mass, the Peons came on, and we turned in full retreat.

Hardy and I stopped and turned back to fire again, but my weapon clicked. I realized I had not followed ammunition protocol. As I ducked behind a doorway, I pulled another clip from my belt and reloaded the weapon. When I looked up, I saw Hardy looking at me, shaking his head dismissively. 'Darn it to heck,' I thought. I fouled up in front of the Sergeant.

There was no time to discuss the issue, as once more, we fired. I lost track of how many I killed, but it was clear there was no way we were going to win. We fell back further, fighting all the way as our comrades fell one by one until it was only myself and Hardy left in that area of the ship. That's when the miracle happened. I had been praying for one, and God answered my call. The Peons started to fall back. I looked at Hardy, but he was as confused as me. "What's going on, Sergeant?" I asked nervously, but he shook his head and shrugged.

"I don't know, Dobson." He edged forward as the last of the Peons disappeared down the corridor.

The intercom came on, and the captain's voice could be heard, "Lieutenant Plural, stand down. Purple sky, I repeat, purple sky. Stand down"

"What does he mean by 'purple sky,' Sarge?" I asked, but Hardy just shook his head again, not knowing the answer. While reading Mr. Phelkar's account, I found out that it meant that it was a genuine order and not something said under duress. Only then did I notice that Hardy had a bloody wound on his shoulder.

Once more, the intercom crackled into life, "Lieutenant Plural, confirm that you have stood down. Report to the cockpit."

"Stand down, confirmed." We heard her reply aggressively.

We met up with the other surviving marines just as Lieutenant Plural came into the area, "Get Tracker to download Doctor Archer and see to the wounded. Then start racking and stacking our dead in the cargo hold."

"What about the Peon's dead and wounded?" A Marine asked.

"Stick them out the airlock," she barked, heading away from him.

"The wounded, Ma'am?" He inappropriately questioned.

"I don't like repeating myself, Reeves," She said, not looking back. "They don't take prisoners in space, so neither do we."

We started to see to our own wounded, but there was a stunned silence when the captain's message that the United States had surrendered and that the war was officially over came over the tannoy. We just stood there in disbelief. "Sarge, come on. You need to get that seen to." I said at last, referring to his wound.

"It's fine." He stared at me, and I shrugged it off. If he wanted to bleed out, that was his affair. It was only then everything started to sink in as I looked around at the carnage throughout the ship.

As Hardy took over the organization of the dead, I slipped away to check on Kelsey. I headed back to the corridor where it all began. I found her sitting with her back and head against the wall, very much alive. "Hey," I said as I approached her. She opened her eyes and looked up at me with a start.

"Hey, Dodgson." She said weakly.

I looked her up and down with a frown. I could not see anywhere that she was injured. "Where did they get you? "

She pointed up to her left shoulder. "Right here."

I crouched down beside her and took a look. Indeed there was a bullet hole in the edge of her uniform, but the projectile had barely grazed her. I had injured myself more seriously with a paper cut. I looked at her with incredible distain. "This is barely a graze."

"It hurts like fuck," she snapped at me.

"Then we best get you to the med bay, hadn't we," I said curtly.

As I started to help Kelsey up, I heard a moan nearby. I left her and told her to wait while I checked on this other survivor.

I looked down at a Peon, trying to rise up. He was clutching a gut wound, and as he managed to turn himself over, he looked up at me, and his eyes widened in terror. I looked down at the scum with contempt. We had officially surrendered but could I just walk away or, even worse, help him? I unfastened my holster and slipped out my snap pistol. "Pardon me, Monsieur." I could not speak French, but I knew a few words. With him crying, "non, non, non," I let off a round right into his face. He slumped back. Behind me, Kelsey gasped. I looked back at her and shook my head in disbelief. "Come on, get up," I said, pulling up her arm.

As she got to her feet, she looked at me, terrified. "What are you going to say about me?"

I shrugged. "Nothing. I am not an officer nor an NCO. It is none of my business." Oh, but I so wanted to make it my business.

We made our way to the medical base. Doctor Archer, whose name I did not know until long after she died, looked up at us as we entered. She was surrounded by wounded with every bunk in use. "Unless your dying, you're going to have to wait outside. "

"I am unharmed," I said. "It is my colleague here that requires assistance. "

"Well, she can wait outside, and you can help me. They did not download my nurses."

I slipped off my jacket, and for the next twenty minutes, I helped clean up wounds and applied bandages while the doctor attended to the more serious cases. I then tagged the ones who had died while receiving treatment.

There was a scuffling outside and I heard Kelsey cry out, and someone shouted at her in French.

The door burst open, and two men in light blue Peon uniforms holding rifles stepped into the room, pushing Kelsy ahead of them. A man nearby tried to get up from his bunk, and I realized it was Sergeant Hardy, who I would find out had collapsed from his wounds. A Peon pointed his gun toward him, and he lay back down. They barked orders at us, but none of us could understand the words, but as they walked around the room, checking the dead and wounded for weapons, it was clear we were told not to resist.

When one of them came up for me, he looked me up and down with a lewd sneer. He stared at my chest. I had developed a rather ample breast which was somewhat an impairment as a marine and frequently drew glances from less eloquent males and some females. He reached down, and for a moment, I thought he was going to touch me somewhere inappropriately, but he just removed my snap pistol from its holster. He muttered something at me, and his companion laughed. However, they headed back to the door with the other Peon turning back to say something and, with his hands, indicated we were to stay in this room. I stood staring at the door, fuming in anger. "Come on, private. We still have work to do," Doctor Archer said to me, and we continued working with the injured.

I was surprised when Lieutenant Plural entered with Mr. Phelkar and another Peon guard a little while later.

"I need more help. Tell these idiots that I need my team downloaded." The doctor demanded.

"They're not going to listen. They're going to have you upload any wounded." Lieutenant Plural replied disinterestedly.

"Half of these men have shrapnel with them. They can't be uploaded until I remove it."

"Do the best you can, doctor." Lieutenant Plural sounded frustrated. "However, first, I need you to take a bullet out of my stomach."

"Sorry, Lieutenant, you're still walking. You have to wait your turn. I have other priorities of a more serious nature."

"I really must insist, doctor. You need to remove a bullet, and you need to do it behind that curtain there." She indicated the privacy screen of a small examination cubicle.

The doctor was about to object but realized Lieutenant Plural was up to something.

"Come in then, Lieutenant."

The doctor led Lieutenant Plural behind a screen, and the guard made to follow, but Mr. Phelkar stopped him and said something in French. The guard headed out, and I could no longer hear the conversation as they whispered.

The doctor looked mad as she stepped out from behind the curtain and headed off to where she stored her meds.

A female Peon officer entered and, after looking around, she headed over to Mr. Phelkar.

She spouted French at him, then spat into his face. I made to move toward them, but Kelsey grabbed my arm.

The Peon continued shouting at him in French until the doctor went behind the curtain again, and she followed her in.

Then it all happened so fast as Lieutenant Plural stepped out from behind the curtain.

"Hey, you," She called to one of the guards. "Something is wrong with one of your people here."

The guard stepped over, and as he passed Lieutenant Plural, she shoved an injector into his neck. As he went down, she pulled his pistol from its holster and shot the final guard. He fell back over a bunk where Private Mitchell lay, and he snapped the Peon's neck. A cheer went up from the surviving troopers, and Lieutenant Plural had to tell them to "shut up!"

The door opened, and two other guards came in. The one in the lead went down from a shot from Lieutenant Plural. Phelkar jumped on the other, and a struggle ensued. He got him on the floor, and Lieutenant Plural brought her boot down onto his head with a twist.

"You're making a habit of saving my life, Mr. Phelkar." Lieutenant Plural smiled at him as she offered him a hand up.

"It seems to be a mutual arrangement, Lieutenant Plural, but you're most welcome," Mr. Phelkar said with a most charming smile.

Lieutenant Plural turned to the Marine who had been of assistance. "Up for the fight, Private Mitchell?"

He looked delighted but said, "Ma'am, I'd give anything to kill Peons right now, but...." He pulled back the sheet covering his legs and showed us the mangled mess of his knee.

"You always were a shirker, Mitchell." Lieutenant Plural grinned and squeezed his shoulder reassuringly. "Listen to Doctor Archer, and don't grope the nurses."

He laughed. "I'll try not to, Lieutenant, especially as there aren't any."

Lieutenant Plural noticed me. "What is your name, Private?" she asked.

"Dodgson, Ma'am," I told her

"You don't look injured."

"No, Ma'am, I'm not," I replied, hoping she would take me with her.

"You up for a scrap with the Peons?"

"Yes, Ma'am," I replied eagerly.

"Oh no, you don't," the doctor said to her. "If you can't get me my nurses, you can at least leave Dodgson here to help me."

Lieutenant Plural pondered this, and to my great disappointment, she replied, "carry on, Dodgson." Turning to the doctor, she said, "You have her for now."

"Give the Peon fuckers hell from us, Lieutenant," another marine called over to her, and she smiled at him and raised a defiant fist before stepping out of the door.

I glared at the doctor, who now had her back to me, as she moved over to check on Mitchell. Slowly I stepped behind the curtain where Lieutenant Plural had been and looked down where the Peon woman who had spat into Mr. Phelkar's face lay. I stepped over to her and pulled the curtain closed behind me. The woman on the floor opened her eyes just in time to see me place my foot on her throat. She struggled, fear in her eyes as she tried to breathe, and grabbed futilely at my steel-capped marine issue boot, as I pushed down harder. I waited a couple of minutes after she stopped moving to ensure she was dead before removing it.

CHAPTER SIX

ABOARD THE JANGLE BERRY

I often hear people say war is hell. Personally, I don't get it. There is simply nothing better than annihilating the enemies of America.

Although we had technically lost my first battle, the idea that Lieutenant Plural would not accept the surrender and was fighting back had me pumped up and exhilarated. I felt bitter toward the doctor who had stopped me from leaving with someone I now thought of as a gosh darn heroine.

You will know what I mean if you ever have the privilege of meeting Lieutenant Plural. That is, of course, if you are a patriot and love America. Of course, I would eventually come to realize that she was more than a leader, but right then and there, I was just hyped that we were fighting back.

As I stepped out from behind that curtain, I took the opportunity to retrieve my snap pistol from the dead Peon that had taken it from me, and I returned it to my holster. I continued assisting the annoying doctor for probably about another hour and spent that time wondering what Lieutenant Plural was doing. When there was nothing more for me to do, I just stood in a corner and glared at her until she eventually noticed and, in a most condescending way, said to me, "if you want to go, Private Dodgson, just go."

I must admit that a grin crossed my face as she said this, but as I turned to Kelsey and asked, "are you coming?" any joy I felt turned to disgust as, with a terrified look on her face, she shook her head.

So alone, I headed out into the corridor and made my way forward. My snap pistol was out and at the ready. I had no clue where Lieutenant Plural had gone, and I just hoped I would run into her before I ran into the enemy.

No such luck.

"Arrêt!" Someone shouted as I went around the corner, and by the two rifles pointed at me, I concluded it meant 'halt'. The Peons had just been standing in the corridor talking quietly. So quietly that I had not heard them and for a moment, I pondered shooting one of them, but that would have guaranteed my death from the other.

Slowly I raised my hands with the snap pistol still held. He barked another order in his gibberish language, and it did not take a genius to realize they meant 'drop the weapon,' but I just stared at him and shrugged. With the other keeping his rifle pointed at me, he shouldered his own. With his eyes on my weapon, he stepped forward, but just as he reached up for it, a loud kerchang startled all of us.

The ceiling-mounted machine guns started to power up. Fear and panic came upon my opponents as they looked around, terrified. But not for long. I bought the snap pistol down, and with two shots, one in each head, I stood there smiling proudly. I instinctively reached up to feel the security pin that would stop the automated weaponry from targeting me, and it was my turn to panic. I had left my jacket, with the only means of keeping me safe, back in the med center. I turned and started to run but knew I would not make it.

I almost gave up when a young, scared-looking tech came around the corner. "The Peons were panicking so much they just let me go," she told me excitedly. I'm not proud of what I did next, but I'm sure you understand that it was necessary. I have a God-given destiny. She did not. I quickly reached up and pulled the pin from her collar. "What the fuck are you doing?" she said, desperately trying to snatch it back, but I pushed her away hard, and the guns began firing. I turned away and shut out the screams from my mind as I headed back to the med center as if nothing had occurred.

There was silence in the med center. Everyone was trying to work out what had happened. Archer looked up at me as I grabbed my jacket and put it back on. "What the hell is going on out there, Private."

"It would appear Lieutenant Plural has managed to activate the automated defense systems," I said with pride.

"Oh my God, does that bitch know what she's doing?" Archer looked appalled. "There is an extremely high risk of hull punctures. This ship was never designed for it in the first place. The whole installation of it was a screwup."

I wanted to respond to that. I wanted to tell her how pathetic she was worrying about her own life over the potential of victory. However, she was a superior officer. The conventions of rank muted me.

"Better dead than being a Peon prisoner," Mitchell said angrily, and I gave him one of my best smiles.

Everyone began talking nervously about what was going on. We need not have worried. The only living Peon left was that commander, who Lieutenant Plural had locked in the bridge with our captain, who had shown his true colors when he continued to capitulate to the enemy. However, for all intents and purposes, Lieutenant Plural was now in charge of the ship.

Everyone fell silent when the intercom chimed. The confident voice of Lieutenant Jenna Plural came over the line. "Doctor, I need three Marines. What have you got for me?"

Archer looked about and saw Kelsey and me. "I'm willing to release Kelsey Anthony, and you can now have Dodgson, but that's it," the doctor stated firmly.

"I need one more, Doctor. If they can walk and hold a gun, patch them up and send them to me," Lieutenant Plural demanded.

"I'll go." We looked over to see Hardy climbing out of his bunk.

"You still have a bullet in you, Sergeant," Archer argued.

"Slap a patch on it," he sneered, "Plural needs me."

"No, Sergeant, I am not discharging you," the Doctor stated firmly.

He stepped up and glared down at her. "Look at this face, doctor." He pointed at himself. "Do you see it?"

"What is your point, Sergeant?" The doctor asked irritably.

"Does it look like this face gives a flying fuck about whether you discharge me or not?" He was most aggressive.

Archer, although not in the slightest bit intimidated, sighed and turned back to the intercom. "Sergeant Hardy will join you too. However, I will note that he has discharged himself against my advice."

"Noted, Doctor, thank you," Lieutenant Plural replied, and the intercom went off.

"Consider yourself on report for insubordination, Sergeant," Archer told him.

"Yeah yeah," he said, flipping her off as he headed to the door. "Fall in Dobson and Anthony," he ordered, not looking back.

Kelsey looked like she was going to refuse, but I gave her a shove toward the door, and she complied.

Mr. Phelkar already described in detail the plan to take the Jangle Berry, so I will not repeat it here. However, put simply, we were to take a space walk across to that ship and decompress the entire atmosphere by blowing out every air lock simultaneously.

We all met up in the cargo bay, and apart from us, there was Lieutenant Plural, of course, as well as two officers I had not met before, Harlow and Sakamoto.

It was my first day out, and already I had participated in repelling borders, and now I was to participate in an operation to take out a French cruiser. However, it somewhat unnerved me when it appeared that Sakamoto was taking command, not the lieutenant herself. Or rather, I should say major at this stage.

Kitted out in my EMU suit with a heavy Extra Vehicular Maneuver pack on my back (the correct name for what Mr. Phelkar called a 'Jet Pack.')

"Listen up, marines," Sakamoto shouted over the suit comms. "We are going to do this by the numbers. Give me a count off." One by one, the Marines counted themselves off, Lieutenant Plural was number three, and I was number five ."Okay, power up your packs." As the large cargo bay doors opened, I fired up the pack and felt my feet leave the ground. We all moved out into the void.

It was my first time making a spacewalk outside of a simulator, and I would have thought I would be more nervous. But I was quite relaxed as I pushed the jets into the forward position and headed out with the line of marines. We continued forward in formation until Sakamoto came online. "Time to break formation and head for your airlock you have been designated."

Suddenly Sakamoto's voice urgently came online. "You are drifting off course, Major. Do we have a problem?" She did not reply.

I heard the voice of Mr. Phelkar. "She's fine, Lieutenant Sakamoto. Just give me a minute."

"We don't have a fucking minute," Sakamoto yelled at him. "Everyone standby to abort."

"Belay that order," Mr. Phelkar shouted.

"You are out of line, Phelkar!" Sakamoto responded viciously.

"I'm okay," Lieutenant Plural stated determinedly.

"Major, you will keep it together," Sakamoto demanded.

"I got this. Phelkar, you still out there?"

"Give me a sec." The line went dead, and I looked over to see Major Plural was back on course.

I started to grow nervous as I realized our commander had appeared to have lost it momentarily. I could not help but wonder as I realized if that was why Sakamoto had been put in charge. I turned my attention back to the destination and pushed the thrusters forward, increasing my velocity toward the Peon ship. As the airlock I had been designated to came into view, I adjusted my course and started to slow down. The last thing I wanted to do was smack into the hull. My mind went back to my simulator training, and lining myself up, I cut the engines and allowed myself to drift into it. All I could hear was my breathing as I pulled the limpet mines from my belt and began to line them up around the door

Sakamoto came online. "Okay, Marines, they will have already detected us, but you have about three minutes before they will be ready to retaliate, so make it count. Give me a count-off when everything is in place

One by one, the marines counted off, and Sakamoto said, "Okay, on my countdown, set your charges for one minute. That's all the time we have, ladies and gentlemen. Make it count three, two, one, mark."

I set my charges on Sakamoto's mark and put my suit into reverse thrust. I moved my way back out of range, yet I still felt the blast's shockwave. Fortunately, I was prepared for it and adjusted the controls to counter turning into a spin. There was a tense moment as debris flew past me, and I admit I closed my eyes and prayed, hoping my suit would not be punctured. The alarms in my suit did not go off, but there was a moment of panic when Major Plural did not respond to Sakamoto's calls. It was such a relief when I finally heard her voice again. Kelsey had not responded, but that's another story I will get to in a bit.

I had to move fast as the spherical tech robots were already responding and trying to seal the blown-out doorways. I managed to push my way through and landed hard on the deck as I entered the artificial gravity environment. Unlike the Chesty, the Jauréguiberry was bright and well-lit.

"Okay, marines." Sakamoto radioed in. "Once more, by the numbers, confirm you are on board." We all responded except for Kelsey. Suddenly there was a blast of sirens. Sakamoto came back online again. "That signals that the doors are sealed again. Head toward the bridge but stay alert and, for God's sake, don't accidentally shoot each other."

Even in the simulators back in training, I had not been this alone. I felt nervous as I passed through the second door of the airlock. I suddenly spun to my left, looking down the corridors as I heard a French voice. However, I relaxed as I saw it was a repair drone heading toward me.

It was not a combat model and would happily ignore me if I did not engage with it. However, it hung in the air, sensors looking at me for a long moment. Slipping my snap gun from its holster, I waited for to see what it would do, but after some babbling in French, it moved on to the door. Or rather what was left of it.

The gleaming corridor was empty as I made my way down it, heading toward what should be the bridge. I passed several bodies that were lying around in a decompressed mess. I would have felt guilty about how we killed them if it was not for the bodies of fine Americans who lay on board the Lewis Puller. As I moved further down the corridor, I started to pass what looked like a laboratory with large windows looking out onto the corridor. The door was sealed air-tight shut, and I was startled to see two terrified men in white coats looking through the window, almost at levels of panic as they came to terms with what had happened. Seeing me, they came up to the window and started to bang, clearly thinking I might be there to help them. They blathered away in French which, obviously, I could not understand a word of. I stood staring at them through my helmet visor as I wondered what to do. They were enemy combatants, whatever their position was. They were a risk to our mission. I did not know what was in that laboratory or what communications they had, but they had seen me and knew my location, and as far as I knew, they could call for some assistance to take me out.

I walked over to the door and started to press the controls as wide-eyed panic appeared on their faces, and they banged harder and screamed at me. However, the door was locked by some code and would not open for me. The man inside, realizing this, started to relax, but I simply raised my snap gun and fired a single round into the window. It was a rookie mistake. As the air rushed out of the shattering glass, it threw me back against the wall, and I slid down to the ground as my suit alarms began to go off. "Multiple suit punctures. Recommend emergency procedures," my suit's environmental system said, stating the obvious. I pulled a spray of sealant from my hip as I watched the air level go down in my suit's heads-up display. I pulled small pieces of glass out from various places and sprayed the holes with the swiftly hardening substance. The air depletion began to slow. It did not stop entirely, but it was sufficient to get me through the rest of the mission without running out of air. As I climbed back onto my feet, I did not look back into that laboratory. I knew the men were dead. With no more thoughts on the matter, I ventured onward.

Over our comms, Jenna Plural and Sakamoto began discussing an issue about getting the bridge doors open without causing damage. But something else had distracted me. I came across one of the other airlocks we had blown open, and Kelsey was trapped in a tangle of wires. When she saw me, she looked relieved and mouthed silently at me, but I couldn't understand. She tried to point to the side of her head to indicate her communicator was out. She eagerly waited for me to get her out of the mess that she got herself into but grew concerned as I just stood there looking at her. I am sure that I could not hide the contempt on my face. She had betrayed her country twice now with her cowardice, and I believed she would do so again if I allowed it.

I stepped around to the back of her, and as I did, I noticed her smile again, believing I was about to release her from her entrapment. I reached the tube to her air supply and began to unscrew it. Then I realized how silly that was. Maybe the Holy Spirit protecting me made me realize it could be problematic if she were found with her air tube simply detached. I laughed at my stupidity, and, wrapping the tube around my wrist, I yanked it hard. Kelsey started thrashing about, trying to turn around to see what I was doing. I pulled it again, getting a little frustrated now. I had much better things to be doing than this. Kelsey was just a passing irritation. In the end, I grabbed it with two hands. I lifted my foot onto her backside, yanking it at an angle so that even if I could not break the tube thread, I would at least rip the suit itself. For the life of me, I can't remember whether it was the tube or the suit, but it did not come completely off, just sufficient to let the air out like an old bald tyre. I stepped in front of her again and watched as she silently screamed hysterically at me. Most unbecoming of a United States Marine. I could not hear a thing which was kind of disappointing. Then I turned and walked away.

As I joined Major Plural and the others on the bridge, Sakamoto desperately tried to call Kelsey. I said nothing, of course, and positioned myself near the door as Sakamoto headed out to find her. She did, and it was instantly assumed to be an accident. So all good.

Eventually, Major Plural called over to Grant to come and take control of the ship.

When we returned to the Lewis Puller, my services were no longer needed, and I went to my quarters. I carefully packed up Kelsey's stuff and wrote a little note to her parents saying how sorry I was for their loss. After all, it wasn't their fault their daughter was a cowardly piece of treacherous filth. Or maybe it was. Who knows, but I gave them the benefit of the doubt. I popped it in her kit bag so it would be found when her gear was sent back home.

I wasn't surprised when I later learned of the demise of the treacherous captain. Major Plural shot him. It only enhanced my growing respect for Major Plural. He was blatantly a traitor, and no one can possibly deny that.

CHAPTER SEVEN

—— ❖ ——

THE TREACHERY OF STEPHANIE MORRIS

I started to feel part of the team. So it was quite disappointing that I wouldn't be a part of the assault on Phobos. I was aware that I was never part of that plan anyway, but I felt I could do more good down on that moon the Peons infested. We spent quite a bit of time working on repairs. I say working on repairs, but it was more fetching and carrying for technicians than me doing repairs itself. Being in haste, we did not touch the more cosmetic issues such as internal damage, and there were several holes in my quarter's walls looking out onto the corridor. I was able to cover them with a picture of my brother and one of Jesus. I could still hear the comings and goings of people outside my quarters. Tracker successfully repaired the M.E.T. and crewman were downloaded, but all were destined for the Phobos mission. Which meant once they departed for Phobos, I would be all alone except for the Navy personnel.

I was afraid I would be ordered back into the M.E.T., and I kept as low a profile as possible, usually eating meals when no one else was around. One afternoon I stepped into the messroom, not expecting to see anyone there. The first officer, well, the former first officer. To be quite honest, at this stage, I had no idea what rank Stephanie Morris held, and I certainly didn't know she was to become a traitor. I liked her. I did not have a friend since the Lord took his vengeance out on Kelsey. I felt guilty for missing her because I really shouldn't have.

On this particular day, I walked in on Stephanie Morris seated in the mess hall. "My apologies, Ma'am," I said quickly, and I made to step out.

"No, no, come in, marine," she said, beckoning me. I didn't want to. I wanted to go back to my room and wait until she left, but she was an officer even if she had been removed from office. I stepped in and stood in the attention position. "I just made fresh coffee if you want some," she said, smiling at me and indicating the pot on the counter.

"Thank you, ma'am," I said and stepped over to the counter to pour myself a cup. Then I turned with pot in hand and asked, "would you like a refresh, ma'am?"

"Thank you, private...," she said questioningly, pushing her cup toward me, indicating that she wanted to know my name.

"Dodgson, Ma'am," I replied as I refilled her cup. I returned the jug to the coffee maker and stood there holding my cup, unsure of what to do next.

She smiled at me. I noticed a glistening in her eyes as if she had been crying. "Please take a seat, Dodgson."

I did not want to; I just wanted to leave. However, an officer is an officer. So I took a seat in the chair adjacent to her but remained sitting formally. "How are your preparations for the Phobos going?" She asked.

"I understand they are going well. However, I will not be part of that mission, unfortunately." I explained.

"Oh, why not?"

"It was never intended that I be downloaded, Ma'am. I only joined the ship after Lieutenant Plural had put her team together." I felt uneasy telling her about that as I thought her immediate response would be that I should instantly be uploaded again.

"Are you disappointed about that?"

"I must admit I am somewhat." I sighed. "It is what I trained for."

"Well, technically, the war is over now. We should be going home."

I wasn't sure how to respond to this as I did not know the intent behind the statement. Yes, she was technically right. But was she just making a statement, or was she expressing opposition to Major Plural? In the end, all I said was, "yes, ma'am."

"Where are you from, Dodgson."

"Arizona, Ma'am. A town called Sedona."

Morris smiled. "A beautiful town. I went there on vacation once while visiting the Grand Canyon."

"Yes, ma'am, its main industry is tourism," I said formally.

"Do you miss it?"

"I only just joined the ship immediately before this mission. I haven't been gone long enough to miss it yet." I replied.

She pondered my words, and I tried to make out the meaning of her expression as she thought about what I had just said. "So you have not worked with Jenna Plural prior to us leaving Earth on this occasion?" She said eventually.

"No, ma'am."

"Interesting. I will be assuming command of the Lewis Puller during the Phobos mission. Once Lieutenant Plural's team has transferred to the Peon ship, I want you to come and see me on the bridge."

"Yes, ma'am," I said, curious about what she wanted with me. With that, she took her leave, not having even touched the coffee I had poured for her.

"I'll see you then." She said quite warmly.

But as she reached the door, I found myself saying, "ma'am, it's Major Plural now."

"What?" she looked confused for a moment.

"It's Major Jenna Plural now, not Lieutenant."

She hesitated once more before smiling and saying, "yes, Dodgson, of course it is," and with that, she left. I thought nothing more of it.

A couple of days later, Major Plural had her Phobos team transferred to what they now called The Lady Liberty. I felt a pang of disappointment as I watched them cross over to that ship and the airlock sealed. I wanted to watch them depart, but the only window was on the bridge, and I was not yet ready to meet with Lieutenant Morris. I returned to my quarters, took a shower, and wore a fresh uniform before heading to the bridge.

There was a new pilot at the helm. Or rather, I should say an old pilot at the helm, although he wasn't old. I just mean that he was the pilot prior to Stacey Jezebel Grant's joining the ship. I personally thought it was a disgrace that a foreigner should be allowed to accept the position of a United States Officer and command Americans.

Neville Batty was a lively little guy with a cheerful disposition. Instead of returning my salute as I entered the bridge, he remained in his seat and just gave me a little wave like he was passing me in a car on a sunny afternoon in Central Park. Yes, I know you don't drive around Central Park. I just wanted to give it a more colorful metaphor.

Stephanie Morris was seated in the captain's chair and smiled at me as I entered. "Ah yes, Dobson, isn't it?"

"Dodgson, Ma'am."

"Oh yes, Dodgson, sorry."

"Not a problem, ma'am everybody does it."

"That doesn't make it right, Dodgson."

I smiled. Maybe she wasn't as bad after all. She turned her attention back to Batty. "How long is it been since the Lady Liberty departed?"

"About thirty minutes, ma'am."

Stephanie smiled and carefully stepped out of her seat. "You have the bridge, Lieutenant Batty."

"Aye, Ma'am."

"With me, Miss Dodgson." And I followed her out on her heels.

I had no idea where she was taking me and was surprised when we ended up in the M.E.T. room. For a moment, I thought she was going to upload me, but as we stepped inside, I saw there was a young tech who wasn't Helen

Tracker. She had left on the Phobos mission with Lieutenant Plural.

"Private Dodgson, this is Assistant Technician Sinclair." Morris introduced. "Is everything ready, Miss Sinclair?" She asked her.

"Yes, ma'am, I have isolated his matrix."

"Very good, bring him down." As Morris said this, I instinctively closed my eyes to avoid the flash of light. A tall, handsome young man stood before me when I opened them. I turned away quickly to face the wall, completely forgetting that you come out of the M.E.T. buck naked. I listened to his conversation with Morris as she handed him his uniform, and he started to dress.

"What is going on, Stephanie?" He said, sounding confused.

"I have a lot to tell you, Frankie," Morris said.

It turned out that Frank Mitchell was a security officer in the Navy. He had worked aside with Stephanie Morris for several years and had just transferred to the Lewis Puller. Stephanie related the events of the ship's boarding and the United States' surrender.

Naturally, he was in a state of shock. I did not know how to respond to that, and she gave him a moment to adjust as I finally turned round to see the fully dressed, able seaman. I noticed how relaxed Sinclair was as Morris spoke, and I realized that she already knew what was going on. I was completely shocked by what Morris said next.

"Jenna Plural has gone insane. She murdered the captain and assumed control." He looked startled by this news, but I noticed again how Sinclair took that news in her stride.

She was clearly in cahoots with whatever Morris was now up to. "Jenna has left the ship with her cronies. Unless we want to end up dead along with her, we have no alternative but to take action."

Mitchell looked at me and then questioningly at Morris. The fact that he didn't look at Sinclair with the same unspoken question clearly meant he already knew where her loyalties lay. "This is Dodgson," Morris said. "She's new and a loyal United States Marine Corps member. I have brought her in as my personal guard, as I do not know how the crew will respond. "

Mitchell smiled at me and extended a hand. I maintained my composure, not wanting to give away my thoughts at this stage. To be honest, I was still trying to work everything out in my head. I smiled warmly and took his hand. "Hi there, Dobson. I am Chief Petty Officer Frank Mitchell. I'm the ship's head of security, and I look forward to working with you." He was so charming and kind, but then the devil is the great deceiver, isn't he?

"Likewise, chief," I said with my sweetest smile.

He turned to Morris. "Are there any of her people still remaining?"

"Well, there is Rock Harlow, the chief engineer. However, he is quite elderly now. I doubt he put up much of a fight. I don't know why Jenna got him posted to this ship. He should have retired years ago."

"Yeah, the most you'll get from Harlow is a few grunts of disapproval at the worst." Sinclair chuckled.

"Neville Batty is quite a wild card. He worked with Jenna for the last four years, but Stacey Grant replaced him as chief pilot at her instruction, so who knows? He does seem enamored by her."

"It is more like Neville is thinking with his dick." Sinclair grinned. "He has the hots for anyone with a slim waistline, and there's no denying Jenna Plural is probably the hottest thing he's ever seen."

"Oh really?" Morris said with mock indignation.

Mitchell grinned at her, and she stepped up close to him, and I thought for a moment she was going to kiss him. However, he glanced over at me, and then so did she, somewhat embarrassed. She stepped back. I did my best to act as if I had not noticed anything, and Morris smiled appreciatively at me for it.

I didn't know what I had walked into at this point, but I really didn't like it. Not only did it appear that Stephanie Morris was about to betray Major Plural, but she was also fraternizing with an enlisted man. How disgusting!

"There is some bad news." Sinclair said, "Tracker has the computer systems encoded with an algorithm that is way beyond my ability even to understand, let alone override. I did ponder talking to her about the situation because I believe it may have been possible to persuade her to throw in with us. I know she has issues with Jenna's ethics. However, Plural kept us so busy I didn't get a chance to be alone with her."

Morris sighed. "Well, it's academic now, as Tracker is on Phobos and will remain there until the Peons pick her up." I couldn't help but audibly react to this. Morris turned toward me. "Yes, I know it absolutely sucks, but I have a duty to those I can actually help. Plural will lead these people to their deaths, and it's my duty to ensure I can save as many as possible from her insanity."

It was far too dangerous at this point for me to disagree. I decided to see how this would play out and simply replied, "I understand, ma'am. It's just I like Helen Tracker." Heck, I didn't even really know Helen Tracker. Which was kind of ironic considering how well I would come to know her in the following months.

They seemed to accept what I said as Mitchell grinned at me. "It's impossible not to like Helen Tracker. She is such a sweetheart. However, the commander here is right. It's not like we can take on Jenna Plural's marines even if we wanted to. For all her failings, her reputation as one of the greatest tacticians ever is not without merit."

"Okay, let's do this." Morris steeled herself. "You and Dodgson go to the armory. Make sure you at least have sidearms at all times. Sinclair and I will head up to the bridge and meet you there."

The four of us headed out, and we went in separate directions. I followed behind Mitchell as we made our way to the Armory. I considered taking him out then and there. Step up behind him, an arm around his neck, a quick twist, and drop him. Adios mother fornicator. But what then? Go up to the bridge with a snap pistol blazing away? If Batty sided with Morris, we were up the Colorado River without a paddle. We only had two pilots. Batty was already the backup as the Jezebel was aboard the Lady Liberty.

No, this was a game of patience, and I needed to see where this was going. Mitchell cheerfully chatted with me and asked me questions about my background, which I politely answered in my usual sweet and friendly manner.

Being chief of security, he had the access codes to the armory, and we went in. Now, this was Nirvana to me. To be surrounded by all these tools of divine retribution, I just wanted to hug each and every rifle, explosive, and blade. Alas, Mitchell removed two snap pistols from a rack and handed me one with a spare clip. "These are only for last resort, Dobson," he said very carefully. "The whole objective here is to save lives, not take them."

"Yes, chief," I said, and to be quite honest, he was absolutely right. The sanctity of the patriotic American's life was absolute. Together, we headed up to the bridge.

Chapter Eight

━━ ❂ ━━

Working for the Enemy

Stephanie Morris was back in the command seat, and Sinclair stood at her side. "The lady liberty has advised us they have successfully disabled the Phobos minefield," Sinclair advised him.

"Excellent," Mitchell said as he slipped into the copilot chair next to Batty. "Hey Neville, how are you doing, buddy?"

"Hey Mitch," Batty gave him a beaming smile. "Good to see you, bud. It's been a while."

Mitchell laughed. "Hey, it's only been a day for me. I'm starting to think I'll spend the rest of my life in an M.E.T.."

Batty chuckled. "Yeah, I know what you mean. Ever since Stacey took my place as the senior pilot, I have felt like a spare part in storage."

"We should put in for a transfer to a bigger ship when everything is over, so we don't spend so much time not existing." Mitchell laughed and then turned to Morris and asked, "any chance of any coffee, Ma'am?"

Morris smiled at him, a little too warmly for my liking, and then looked up at me and said, "Would you be a dear? "

Be a dear? Holy moly, was she serious? However, I nodded, returned her smile, and said, "yes, ma'am."

I headed back down to the mess, where I made a pot of coffee and pondered if there was anything I could put in it to take them out. I did not know how far this ran deep, and I could not risk harming Batty if he was a patriot. So, disappointed, I returned to the bridge with a tray of mugs and a pot of regular coffee, poured it out for everyone in turn, and handed it out like a steward.

Morris dismissed Sinclair and me, asking us to report back in a couple of hours. As we both left, I walked alongside Sinclair and could not help but notice in my peripheral vision that she kept looking up at me. Eventually, I said, "is something on your mind, Sinclair?"

"Sorry," she said sheepishly. "I was just thinking...you know." Her voice trailed off, and she looked uncomfortable.

I didn't know. I stopped walking and turned to face her. "Say what you want to."

"Please call me Paris. "

I frowned, "why? "

She looked surprised at my question and then laughed a rather delightful little laugh. "Because that's my name. Paris Sinclair."

"Oh, I see. I'm sorry." Then I added, "that is rather an unfortunate name given our circumstances don't you think?"

She laughed. "You're not the first to mention that." Now I understood why she was a traitor. No true American would ever call their daughter Paris or any other French name. "Look," she said, steeling herself. "You know, umm, you're kind of cute. I was wondering, umm, after all this is over, maybe we could have a drink together or something."

My reaction to this was confusing. Usually, my first reaction would be utter repulsion that anyone would expect me to enter some sort of same-gender relationship. But standing in front of me, looking so nervous and sweet at the same time, I felt the desire to pull her to me and give her a great big hug. Impure thoughts about this young woman entered my head, for even I must admit that she was a sweet and attractive girl. What I said was, "I appreciate the compliment, Paris, and I'd be happy to have a drink with you as friends. But anything more is not really my inclination." Yet part of me wanted more than that. I had experienced attraction to other women before, and the sinfulness of it bothered me.

She looked disappointed, but she smiled. "That is possibly the sweetest rejection I have ever had." She laughed. She had such an adorable laugh, and I was kind of saddened that I would eventually have to rip it off her face.

I placed a reassuring hand on her shoulder and said, "don't worry. I took it as a compliment." I then went to my cabin, telling her I would see her later. The first thing I did was wash my hands thoroughly and sanitize them as if she had contaminated me.

I was angry at myself for my feelings of attraction to her. I briefly wondered if a demon had got into my soul but eventually put it down to the temptations of the great deceiver. If thoughts like this continued, I realized I would have to take drastic action to stop my ability to be sexually aroused. All of this was not about me. It was about my calling. I decided that I should fast for a day to clear my body in my mind and deal with the challenges I faced. I spent the next couple of hours reading my Bible and praying until it became time for me to return to the bridge.

Sinclair was already there, and there was heightened tension emanating from both Morris and Mitchell. As I stepped in, Morris advised me, "Plural has landed. They are engaging the enemy, and the Liberty is on course for a mission to get a new air supply."

"So the time has come?" I asked. My hand casually slipped down to my holster and over the grip of my snap pistol, getting ready to draw it should I need to.

"Let's let Stacey get further away before we do anything," said Mitchell, and Batty looked up confused, but when no one said anything to him, he kind of shrugged and looked back at his console.

We stood there in silence forever, but it was probably only an hour. Mitchell turned to Morris, and she nodded to him. He got out of his chair and casually stood behind Batty, and I watched him slip his hand down to his snap gun. I moved to the doorway so no one could see me unless they turned around, and I gripped my snap gun, too, ready to pull it out should he do anything to harm Batty.

"Fire up the engines, Mr. Batty, and bring us about," Morris ordered, and he automatically complied. It was not a pilot's place to question the commanding officer, but what she said next made him turn around. "Plot a course for Earth and set us on maximum speed."

He spun around in his seat. "Are you sure, ma'am?" He asked with wide, confused eyes.

"You heard the captain, Mr. Batty. Please don't question her authority," said Mitchell, but he relaxed as Batty frowned, then shrugged and turned to plot the course.

"Course set in. ETA seven weeks and four days."

"Thank you, Mr. Batty," Morris said cheerfully.

And there it was. There was no doubting it now. Stephanie Morris had just abandoned Major Plural and her marines on Phobos and was about to turn us over to enemy forces. My mind raced on what to do. I did not even know who among the crew I could trust anymore.

"Mr. Mitchell, would you please give Mr. Batty that frequency we discussed so he can call her up," Morris ordered.

Mitchell slipped a piece of paper out of his pocket and slid it across the console to Batty. He looked at it, then looked up at Mitchell, then at Morris, and then patched the call to the frequency provided.

"Taggart here." Came the voice of an unfamiliar woman over the radio.

"Corporal Taggart, it is good to hear your voice again," Morris said cheerfully,

"Likewise, Lieutenant. I was starting to worry I wouldn't hear from you. How is everything going over there?"

"We have taken the Lewis Puller," Morris said with pride. "Now it's up to you to take The Liberty. Did you manage to recruit any of your colleagues into our mission?"

"No, ma'am. I am on my own, but I have incapacitated two of the marines with me. That leaves Grant, her tech, and Pentauk."

"I would rather there was no bloodshed, but if you have no choice, you will have to take out Stacey Grant and the others. Are you willing to do that?" There was a barely audible laugh as Taggart replied, "Willing to take out Stacey Grant? Hell, I'd actually enjoy it."

"Only if absolutely necessary, Miss Taggart," Morris instructed. "You want to place her under arrest if at all possible. Do we understand each other?"

"Yes, of course," Taggart said with frustration. "I will call you again once I have control."

As you can probably tell, I'm not the biggest fan of that Jezebel Stacey Grant, but at least at this point, I knew she was as loyal as any foreigner could be. There was no way I wanted her to be killed. Well, at least not back then. That would obviously change, but she was on my side right now, and I possibly needed her. Desperate times and all that. However, I was in an impossible situation. Even if I took out Morris, Mitchell, and Sinclair right now, that would not stop this Taggart.

"Okay, what the fuck is going on?" Batty made to jump out of his seat, but Mitchell pushed him back down again from the shoulder.

"Trust me, Mr. Batty, I am trying to save all our lives," replied Morris.

"Killing one of my best friends doesn't sound like trying to save lives," Batty protested. I assume he referred to Grant, but I couldn't imagine her having friends. At least not loyal American ones.

"That will be the decision of Stacey herself. No harm will come to her if she stands down and recognizes my command," Morris replied. "But I must consider the greater good of many more lives I could save."

"And Mr. Batty," said Mitchell. "I don't want to hurt you, but you have already laid in the course for the Earth, and who's going to control the ship will not become a problem for seven weeks. We can do without you, but we'd rather not."

"This is fucking bullshit," he muttered, turning back to the controls with resignation. He almost immediately looked back up at Morris. "We have a call coming in from the liberty."

"Put it on speaker," Morris ordered.

That crudely accented voice I would eventually grate on my nerves came over the tannoy system. "This is Stacey Grant of the USS Lady Liberty, to the USS Lewis Puller. Do you read me?"

Mitchell looked back at Morris, concern on his face. She sighed dejectedly and shook her head slowly before responding. "This is Mason. Go ahead, Miss Grant."

"I don't know what you're playing at, mate, but your little coup here has just failed." The was a sigh from Jezebel before she continued. "I want you to listen very carefully."

93

Morris did not respond, so Grant repeated. "Are you listening?"

"Yes!"

There was a longer pause, and then suddenly, the sound of a snap gun going off, followed by a dull thud before the Australian's voice came back filled with frustration. "Do you know what that was, Stephanie? That was the former Corporal Taggart dying. I did not want to do that, but I do not have the resources here to take prisoners." I could not help but smile, but I hid it quickly before anyone noticed. Batty was less desreet. "You go, Stacey," he muttered with a grin.

"Listen to me, Stacey," Morris said steadily and firmly, but I could see her shaking slightly. "You have to know that Jenna Plural is power crazy. She's out of her freaking mind. Do you really think she and a handful of United States marines could take on the whole solar system? Do you think you're going to fly the Lewis Puller into Canberra and liberate Australia? Listen to how stupid that is."

"You are probably entirely correct," Stacey replied. "However, I'd rather go out taking as many of those fuckers with me than stick my head between my knees and kiss my arse and the arse of the nearest Peon." There was a pause. "We will be coming for you. That is something I am sure will be Jenna's first order upon her return." And with that, the line went dead.

I looked at Morris, who had her elbow resting on the arm of the chair and was biting her thumbnail, thinking out what to do next. "If she finds a way to get Plural off that moon, they will be coming after us," Mitchell said urgently. "We cannot outrun the Liberty, *and* she will have an almost complete company of United States marines with her."

"All we can do is hope Grant is not successful with her mission to the Peon space station," Morris muttered.

"That's leaving a lot to chance, Stephanie. We have to find a way to ensure that they don't come after us." Mitchell insisted.

Morris sighed, looked up at the ceiling, then dejectedly, she looked to Batty. "Call up the Peon space station she is heading for."

Batty turned in his seat and raised his eyebrows. "Excuse me?"

"You heard me, Mr. Batty. Please, let's not make this worse than it already is."

Batty turned back, tapped in the frequencies, and violently hit the control. "You have an open line, Captain," He said to the captain with deliberate contempt.

"This is the USS Lewis Puller to European base blah blah." Obviously, she didn't say 'blah blah,' but I can't remember whatever silly name they had for it. Someone responded in French, but moments later, someone speaking pretty reasonable English for a Peon came online. "How can we help you, mademoiselle?" Although the words were polite, there was clear suspicion in his voice. There may have been a peace called, but that didn't end twenty years of suspicion.

"This is Captain Stephanie Morris of the USS Lewis Puller. There is a ship headed toward you with the transponder codes for a ship in your fleet called the Jangle

Berry." She said the proper French name for the ship, of course. "It is under the control of an Australian renegade. She intends to take your base by force in order to obtain your supplies."

There was a pause before he replied. "If this is so, then why would you tell me? You are American."

"This is a rogue element. This is not an officially sanctioned United States action."

Again there was another pause before he reluctantly said, "very well, we will take it under advisement."

Morris was about to say something else, but Batty advised her they had cut the line. "I felt dirty doing that, but it was for the best." She muttered. Standing behind her, I struggled not to show the bare unadulterated anger seething through my body.

As time passed after communicating with Stacey, I almost fell into despair and prayed constantly, but no answer came. I started to think my Lord had abandoned me. Maybe because of those evil impure thoughts and attraction to Paris Sinclair. He had not abandoned me, and it was what happened a few days later that I saw the purpose my Lord had for me.

I was sleeping late that day. Any former military protocol had gone out the window, and no one assigned me any duties. However, I woke with a start when Sinclair came banging on my door. I did not want to excite her by seeing me in my pajamas, so I pulled on my dressing gown and wrapped it tightly around me before I opened the door. There was no greeting. She just blurted it out. "Somehow,

Plural has escaped Phobos with the help of Stacey Grant. The Liberty is coming after us."

My heart skipped an excited beat, but I hid my joy well. "Will they catch up before we get to Earth?"

"According to Batty, they will overtake us in just a few more days. Apparently, they have been following for quite a while, but he managed to hide their signature from us, the little shithead."

Good old Neville Batty. American heroes come in all shapes and sizes and from all walks of life. To be a hero, you don't have to be a frontline combat veteran. But it helps.

CHAPTER NINE

━━ ● ━━

JUSTICE IS SERVED

An opportunity to take out Morris still did not occur, and I became increasingly frustrated as the next few days passed. There were many meetings held that I attended. Sinclair reported she had managed a workaround, and it was finally decided that they would start downloading the remaining marines to repel any attempt to board from The Lady Liberty.

So on my way back to the quarters, I stopped off at the M.E.T. room, opened up the control panel, and pulled out a couple of wires, hoping I wasn't going to cause harm to those inside. However, desperate times call for desperate measures, as I have said before.

Hopefully, the traitors would think it was related to the previous damage caused during Lieutenant Plural's takeover of the Chesty.

As The Liberty started to pull in for the attack, Sinclair went to begin the downloads. She quickly reported the fault to the captain, so I kindly offered to go down and help her.

She was flustered as she tried to work out what was wrong. When she opened up the casing, she frowned. "Fucking hell," she cursed. "This isn't accidental someone has sabotaged this."

"Can you fix it?" I asked, hoping for a negative answer.

"Oh, this will take just two minutes," she said brightly.

"I was hoping you were not going to say that." I sighed softly.

She turned to face me with a confused expression. "Huh?"

I slammed the palm of my hand onto her face and hit her head against the wall with considerable force. Unfortunately, I couldn't shoot or stab her because that would leave a nasty mess they could find.

She screamed in pain and fear, and I covered her mouth and slammed her head several more times before realizing that if I split her skull open, that would make a mess too. She looked up at me with shock and tried to say something that sounded like, " why?" but I can't honestly be sure. I dragged her down onto the ground as she thrashed about, trying to kick and scratch me, but I managed to get her face down and knelt a knee upon her back, and with a sharp yank of her head, I heard the sound of bone and cartilage cracking in her neck.

One down, two to go.

I dragged her body out of the room, and half lifting and half carrying, I took her to a seldom-used storage closet. At least it wouldn't be used until this situation was resolved. Ironically, it turned out no one ever found her, and I would later put her body into the garbage regularly ejected into space.

With justice served on Paris Sinclair, no backup would be arriving from the M.E.T.. I headed back up to the bridge

Morris looked clammy and pale, which both delighted and disgusted me. "How is Sinclair doing?" She asked me.

"She seems to be doing okay," I replied. "However, she said she couldn't concentrate with me there and asked that everyone should leave her alone."

"Get back down there and tell her I want a solid timeline on when we will be able to download our troops. I nodded and went to sit in the mess room for ten minutes, drinking a cup of coffee before returning to report my findings. I walked in just as she was finishing a conversation with Major Plural on the radio

"You have had your chance to surrender, Morris," Major Plural said. "Your time is up. When we next meet each other, my face will be the last one you see. Liberty out."

The eyes of myself, Batty, and Mitchell were all on Stephanie Morris. She was visibly shaking now, but no commands came from her voice. "What are your orders, captain?" Mitchell asked.

A deathly silence hung aboard the ship until a clang rang through the ship, and those of us standing almost lost our balance.

"Wow, Stacey is just going to bounce grapple on us. Color me impressed," laughed Batty, but neither Stephanie nor Mitchell were amused.

"We have to get out of here, Mitchell. Take our chances in a life pod. Jenna is not going to let this go. We are both dead if she gets back aboard this ship. " She looked at me. "You should come too. I don't think 'I was only obeying orders' will cut any ice with that psychopath."

I nodded and followed both Mitchell and Morris out of the bridge.

If I was going to do something, I was severely running out of time. I did wonder if I should just wait for Major Plural to board, but if she got into an escape capsule, there was no way the two ships could disentangle in time to pursue her, and there was no way I was going to let her walk away from this.

I only had as long as it took to walk from the front of the ship to the back to do something. I asked God to give me a sign, and in response, Major Plural's voice came on the ship-wide intercom.

"This is Major Jenna Plural of the Lady Liberty. We already have control of the Chesty, and I am ordering you to stand down. This is your chance to be patriots, ladies and gentlemen. Stand down and place Stephanie Morris under arrest."

This was it. I removed my snap pistol from my holster as we turned a corner. I started to raise it toward the back of Morris' head, but as bad luck would have it, Mitchell turned around to say something to me just as I was doing so. His eyes widened, but at the same time, he swiped my arm, and the snap gun fired off into the wall. Morris barely glanced back and ran around the corner. But Mitchell grabbed my arm and banged it against the wall until I dropped the firearm. I tried to bring my knee up into his groin, but he managed to step back without letting go of me. He then twisted my arm, causing me to turn around, and had every intention of breaking it.

I managed to bring the heel of my boot back against his shin. Hardly enough to do anything other than give him a nasty bruise but sufficient to distract him momentarily. I broke free, spun around, and punched him squarely in the jaw. I don't know who it hurt more, him or me, but the fight was on.

I followed up with a head butt breaking open his nose, but in an unexpected move, his hands went for my neck and latched on. It is the automatic instinct of a human to go for the hands that are choking it. And I did just that. A fruitless and pointless move as I began to soundlessly gag under the pressure of his thumbs as they were squeezing the life out of me. Fortunately, my training came to me, even as he forced me to the ground and landed on top of me. With all the strength I could muster, I rammed my forefinger into his eye and kept it going up to the knuckle. The weird sucking sound as I pulled my finger out was barely audible above his screams. He clutched at his face, and I tried to heave him off of me as blood and slime poured from his eye socket down onto my face.

It took a while to get him off me, and I scrambled up to my feet as he flailed out at me. I brought my boot down onto the side of his head, stamping down harder and harder until he fell silent and stopped moving. He was dead, but I didn't know it, for I had no time to check.

I pulled his security cuffs from his belt, snatched up my gun, and ran faster than ever. My old drill Sergeant would have had nothing to complain about this time.

Morris was climbing into one of the escape pods as I entered the bay. I stepped up to her, my snap pistol raised. "Please stop what you're doing, ma'am. Major wants you alive, but I will shoot you if I have to."

She turned around and raised her hands. "What made you change sides? "

"I never switched sides. There has always only been one side, which is the side that will fight for America and not bow down to the satanic forces of the European Union." I admit I was most undignified in my anger; I was firing spittle at her.

"Oh my God, you are as insane as she is," Morris muttered.

"Insanity is thinking you could get away with this. Victory is and always will be the destiny of the American people. now get out of there." She followed the direction of where I pointed the gun. "Turn around and hands against the wall. Move so much as an inch, and I will shoot you."

"That would probably be better than whatever Jenna Plural has planned for me."

I shrugged. "Shooting you in the kneecap is not going to kill you," I said coldly, and she quickly complied.

I calmed myself down a bit, trying to compose myself for what I had to do next. I was nervous; my palms were sweaty, and I wiped them on my tunic, which I never usually would do. I remembered the cuffs I took from Mitchell and cuffed her to a pipe. I then went to wash my face and hands before I walked over to the intercom. I took a deep breath, "Batty, would you give me a line to the Lady Liberty, please."

"Why?" He asked suspiciously.

"I have information that Major Plural will want to know." He still didn't trust me, but he complied.

I heard the beep to say the line was open, and very nervously, I said, "This is Private Emma Dodgson. I have Commander Morris in custody, and she's really mad."

There was a pause, and I smiled as I heard cheering and clapping coming over the line, and then *she* spoke to me.

"I think I love you, Private Dodgson," Major Plural said. I blushed and wanted to squeal like a cheerleader whose daddy had just given her a new car.

"Um, I guess that's appreciated, ma'am," I said, trying to sound professional.

"Clear the portside. We are coming aboard."

"Aye, ma'am."

Eventually, Hardy would arrive and take charge of the prisoner. He was a lot rougher with her than I would have been, and I noticed he had a big roll of cable over his shoulder and wondered what it was for. As I trotted on behind them, I admit I found it quite exciting.

We went into the cargo bay and were soon joined by Major Plural and Mr. Phelkar. Stephanie Morris stood in the center of the room, her hands bound behind her back. She struggled to maintain her composure, but the terror was clear in her eyes. Major Plural walked straight up to her and slapped her hard around the face. "You disgust me."

It was such a joy to see my leader, the future of the American people, so strong, so powerful, and so in charge. Whatever my feelings were for her before, I now realized how much I adored her, and as she slapped Morris, I could not help but give a little gasp of pleasure. Mr. Phelkar, always the perfect gentleman, thought the scene was bothering me and turned to me and whispered, "do you want to wait outside?" I declined his kind offer and stood resolutely, ensuring that I made no more such outbursts.

"Look, Jenna," Morris said between anguished sobs. "You don't need to do this. Let's just talk about it. Let me out of here, and I will follow you anywhere you want. I will accept your authority."

Major Plural folded her arms and paced up and down in front of her. "You are a complete coward, aren't you?" She said with bile in her tone. "You think I will just sit back and forget your crimes?"

Morris began visibly shaking, and Major Plural suddenly stepped back in horror as a wet patch appeared at her crotch. She was so afraid she had peed herself. She defaced the uniform of a United States Marine. A uniform, I should say, she should never have been allowed to wear.

"String her up," The Major instructed Hardy.

Hardy nodded. He threw the cable over a beam in front of the former First Officer, and I saw it had been formed into a slipknot.

"Let's leave him to it," Mr. Phelkar said to me, but Major Plural thought he was talking to her.

She shook her head, "You can leave if you want to, but I promised Morris that I would be the last thing she sees, and I won't be faithless."

And there was no way I would miss seeing this foul traitor dispatched. Tears streamed down Stephanie Morris's face, and I went to help her to stand as Malcolm put the noose around her neck. She looked at me with eyes pleading with me to help her.

"Raise her slowly," Major Plural commanded and moved to stand directly in front of her, her hands behind her back and legs astride. Malcolm nodded and pulled her slowly up about half a foot from the ground. As the tips of her toes left the ground, Stephanie Morris struggled with her legs, unable to do anything with her bound hands. Her face quickly turned red as the air supply was cut off. Phelkar, a sensitive soul, turned away, but Major Plural and the rest of us watched.

We remained there in silence for several minutes as Morris continued to struggle. I was so disappointed when Major Plural sighed and pulled out her sidearm. She shot her squarely in the chest. She really did not deserve that mercy. Morris momentarily stiffened and then fell limp as the front of her shirt turned red. Major Plural remained, staring at her for a full minute. Then, turning away, she strode to the door without looking back, muttering the order, "throw her out of an airlock."

As I watched her go, I realized she was our new savior. I couldn't possibly comprehend the rhyme behind her reason. For I was not worthy and simply honored to be of service to her.

Chapter Ten

⟶ ⊗ ⟵

Celebrations and Revelations

I was summoned to Major Plural's office the next day. I wanted to change into a fresh uniform, but with the last few days' events, I did not have any. I was pretty much wearing my last decent set. As I raced up to her office, my heart was pounding. What could she possibly want? Had they found the body of Sinclair? I was yet to dispose of it at this point. I often wonder why that bothered me so much. I could certainly justify killing her. I guess it was just becoming a habit.

When I entered her office, I stood at attention until she permitted me to stand down, and she rose from behind her desk with a big smile as she moved around to stand before me. "Lieutenant Dobson, isn't it?"

"Dodgson, ma'am."

"Oh, I'm sorry, Private Dodgson. I wanted to thank you for your sterling work. Were you also responsible for Mr. Mitchell?"

"He gave me no choice, ma'am. He tried to stop me from arresting Lieutenant Morris."

Major Plural laughed lightly and raised a reassuring hand. "Relax, Dodgson. I'm not conducting an inquiry. I wanted to commend you. For conduct above and beyond the call of duty. For bravery in the face of the enemy, but most of all, for making the right decision and showing me your loyalty. I shall not forget that Dodgson." She fixed those bright blue eyes on me. "You are one of my team now, and in time, I hope I will show the same loyalty to you as you have shown me." She offered me her hand to shake, and I took it. It was so soft are smooth. I could only be in the hands of an angel, even more confirming her divine right to rule and lead us through the end of days.

"It is an honor and a privilege, ma'am," I said meekly.

She smiled. "The honor and privilege are mine, Dodgson. You are hereby promoted to the rank of corporal." She returned to her desk, and sitting back, she arched her fingers and stared at me a while longer, "Mr. Phelkar requires a personal assistant, not a job I would usually give to a combat veteran, but it's not like we brought clerical staff on this trip, and new circumstances require us to adapt."

"Mr. Phelkar is a very nice man. I will do my best to assist him." I replied.

She smiled again, "I am sure you will, Corporal Dodgson. If you ever need anything, my door is always open. Dismissed." With that, I clicked my heels together and saluted. She stood up and returned the salute, and I left her office.

Working as a clerical assistant would not have been my first choice of position, but I wasn't lying when I referred to Phelkar as a very nice man.

His job was virtually the same as first officer in all but name. He was responsible for working out supplies, crew rosters and enforcing the orders of the Major. The only way he differed from the first officer was that he could not give orders to anyone that hadn't been specifically assigned to work under him. Even then, technically, the orders were that of Jenna Plural being relayed through him.

It kept me busy, and Mr. Phelkar was an absolute delight to work for. He was very kind and considerate and always took out time to check on me. It was nice to have someone make a fuss about me and care about how I was doing.

Slowly the news spread that Major Plural had arranged a rendezvous with all the other patriotic ships of the American fleet that had rejected the treasonous president's surrender. It was all getting rather exciting. Although I was concerned about the rumblings that Major Plural would not be allowed to assume authority.

However, she did not seem too concerned and kindly arranged a celebration for all the crew of all ranks. And it was down to Mr. Phelkar and me to arrange everything. Of course, Mr. Phelkar had no concept of marine tradition, so everything was left to me.

The party kicked off the next day at eight. The Liberty's officer's mess pounded to the music of the latest hits from the USA prior to the capitulation. The first person I saw was Stacey Grant and, of course, the raving alcoholic Jezebel had taken over serving at the bar. As one would expect, she was dressed like a whore in a sleeveless white blouse and ludicrously short pleated tartan skirt. It was embarrassing, to say the least. Helen Tracker was dressed appropriately in bell-bottom grey slacks and a matching button-up vest. All around were the elite of the USA in the best party gear they could keep in their footlocker. Dancing, drinking, and acting like war was a word they had never heard of.

Suddenly the music stopped, and all looked around, wondering why. Suddenly a large beer keg rolled into the room, followed by another. A cheer went up. I noticed Mr. Phelkar looked confused, so I went over to him. "It's the marine tradition ever since the first marines were sent into space. Just watch." And as if on cue Major Plural stepped into the room. Mr. Phelkar looked like his eyes were going to pop out of his head. I started to think that he had a thing for Major Plural. She wore a tight black skirt just above the knee with a matching, almost translucent, sheer collared shirt. Her hair was tied back in a ponytail with a white scrunchie, and a gold chain with a locket hung down on her breast. She sported a pair of three-inch pumps with black stockings and a gold anklet on one ankle. Upon seeing her, we all stopped what we were doing, stood at attention, and saluted.

Major Plural stopped at attention at the entrance and returned the salute. Then the familiar tune of the Marine Hymn began to play, and all but myself and the few navy personnel began to sing. "From the Halls of Montezuma to the shores of Tripoli. We fight our country's battles in the air, on land, and sea." The Star-Spangled Banner immediately followed this. All the while, no one moved from their rigid spot at full attention. Then silence fell, and I watched Major Plural waiting for something to happen. She then lowered her head, everyone followed suit, and Grant began to sing. Some crap about Australia being great. Bleugh!

When she concluded, the attention returned to Major Plural. "Boys and girls of the United States Marine Corps. As your commander, I ask nothing less than your best. On Phobos, you gave me nothing less than your best. So, the beer is on me." It was only then I saw she carried a snap gun. Raising it, she fired once into each keg, and a cheer went up, and marines grabbed up their mugs to get what was called "The Commander's Fill," as it gushed over the floor.

Again as tradition would have it, we had to drink our first tankard in one go, each taking it in turns as the others shouted to us, 'go go go.' Some guy asked me to dance, I don't remember who it was, but it's not particularly important to this story. As we did, I looked to where I saw Mr. Phelkar talking to Stacey Grant. I so hoped that he wasn't getting involved with that Jezebel. She may have been on the side of the Americans, but she was uncouth and still a foreigner. Of course, I know Mr. Phelkar, but there was something different about him, and we had that 'special relationship' with the Brits. It was like he was one of us. Grant, however, was like a fungus that clung to the dark side of the great oak that was the United States of America. An unrepentant drunkard from a culture so uncivilized they even ate their national animal, the kangaroo.

Stacey seemed to catch my eye, grinning, and she said something that Mr. Phelkar, who turned around and looked at me too. I got embarrassed, and I think I blushed slightly and turned away. At least, that is how Mr. Phelkar says I responded. I don't really recall.

Each of us was responsible for joining the patrols, and it was not much later that I had to return to my quarters and get into my uniform again. The ship seemed empty as I strode the corridors with everyone at the party. However, toward the end of my second hour, I heard a voice. A familiar one, and as I walked around the corner, I was startled to see Major Plural Plural standing outside Mr. Phelkar's quarters. She had her heels off, held them in her hand, and looked at him most provocatively. Then she went inside, and the door shut. I did not know what to make of this at first. Somehow I thought Major Plural would be above such things as relationships. However, it was not my place to ever question her. If she chose Mr. Phelkar as a lover, I'm sure my Lord agreed with it. She was surely above the rules of the rest of us.

I had the option to return to the party when I was relieved of duty, but I chose not to return to my quarters on the Lewis Puller.

Mr. Phelkar is probably the sweetest man I have ever met. He is strong and commanding. And that accent was just so dreamy. I cannot deny I had more than a teenage crush on the British diplomat. Working for him was amazing. He literally let me do everything and never questioned how I did it. You would think that having become aware that he was in a relationship with Major Plural Plural, I would have been jealous but that only made him more exciting. Touching him was like touching her.

It happened shortly after that party. Due to the lack of space on board the Lewis Puller, I worked at a small desk in his quarters. I had been alone most of the day and was working late, filling in reports when he returned to his cabin. He looked tired and stressed as I looked up at him from my computer console. "Oh, you're still here," he muttered softly as he walked over to the drinks cabinet and took out a bottle of whiskey. "You really should get along and get some rest."

I smiled up at him. "It's all good, Sir. I enjoy what I do."

He looked at me as he poured his drink, then indicated the glass. "Would you like one?"

"No, thank you, Sir," I said, hoping he would not judge me for it. I don't drink hard liquor.

He smiled and sat in the armchair, which made up the only furniture in the room besides my desk. As he took a sip and swirled the drink in his hand, he studied me carefully. "You are a very attractive young lady, Corporal Dodgson."

I felt myself color up, and my heart went all a pitter-patter as it had once had for Calvin Butler.

"Come and sit over here and take a break," he patted the seat next to him.

Slowly I rose, and although a little unsure, I took my seat next to him.

As I did so, my heart beat faster, and all sorts of unacceptable impropriety ran through my mind unbidden. I sat upright with my knees together and my hands on my lap. He chuckled lightly. "Relax, Dodgson." He said softly, and to my surprise, he placed a hand on my back and rubbed it gently. It felt so good. I looked up at him and smiled softly. My mind was battling the lustful desires that entered my heart. I found I could not look away from him.

This appeared to cause his smile to widen, and he moved his hand down to caress my thigh. Oh gosh! Butterflies danced around my stomach, but they were barely notice-able amid the sensation that was taking place in my more personal areas. We sat there silently as he slowly ran his hand up and down my thigh. Slowly but surely, he gradu-ally moved it to the inner part of my thigh. I knew instantly that I should object, but the words could not come. Then he leaned in and kissed me. It was soft and gentle, and loving. Despite my better judgment, I gave in to it, and my nervousness increased, for I had never been with a man before and had been saving myself for my wedding night.

But everything about this man aroused my desire. He's bearing, his accent, his big brown eyes. But most of all, the knowledge that he had been intimate with the woman that was my hero. To be with him would be like being with her. His hand slid between my legs, and I stiffened As my conscience battled between pleasure and responsibility, I found my breathing getting heavier, and my body tingled with tiny pinpricks. I wanted to say no. I wanted to say stop, but I found myself filled with the evil of bestial desire. I did not know what to do. I did not know where to put my hands, and I felt a little uncomfortable as he kissed me again, and his tongue entered my mouth.

I had never kissed Calvin like that, and it was un-comfortable yet pleasurable at the same time. My breasts heaved up and down with my heavy breaths. He grinned at me as he pulled up my marine issue pullover, and I raised my hands to help him. I felt myself color slightly as he threw the jumper aside and stared down at my breasts encased in nothing but my bra. I looked up at him longingly as he placed his hands on them. He then stood up and, taking my hand in his, pulled me up and against him, his other arm around my waist and pulling me against his body. As he kissed me again, I closed my eyes, but they quickly shot open again as I felt his hand unfasten the back of my bra and release it. "No, Mr. Phelkar, we mustn't do this." I murmured.

"Hush!" he said softly as he pulled the garment off me and tossed it casually aside. "It's okay. I promise you that you're going to enjoy this."

I made to pull away, shaking my head, but he pulled me back to him, and as he leaned in to kiss me again, I was lost. I tentatively tried putting my tongue into his mouth, but it felt just too weird, and I was so uncomfortable not knowing what I should be doing. He stepped back and pulled his shirt off before pulling me back again, and my flesh touched his. I wanted to push him back again, but the sensations coursing through my body were stronger than my resolve. As his hands explored me, they finally slipped down to unfasten my belt, and, thinking I should do the same, I started to unfasten his. As he slipped out of his pants and I mine, I looked down at his exposed parts that stood hard and looked up at me. It was grotesque and disgusting and went some way to curb my ardor. I closed my eyes, not wanting to lose this wonderful sensation, and thoughts of Major Plural once more entered my head. Brave, confident Jenna Plural and my aversion disappeared. As his hands slid down to caress my thighs and buttocks, I imagined it was her touching me. It did not even occur to me the sinfulness of my actions and thoughts, especially about another woman. He lifted me, and instinctively I wrapped my arms and legs around him, his hot member pressing against my belly as he carried me over to the bed in the corner of the room. My eyes were still tightly shut.

I could only see her face and feel her hands and body against me. Jenna Plural. The new savior whom God had chosen to liberate his country and his people. She gently lowered me onto the bed. Her long brown hair nestled against the sides of my face as her body came down on top of me. Then slowly but surely, she violated my inner-most sanctum. I realized then that this was not a sin. This was *her* right to take me and use me in whatever way she pleased. I was hers. The Lord had given me to her, and while it hurt at first, enough to make me gasp in pain, that quickly passed, and the ultimate sensation of pleasure washed over me. I heard her gasp with pleasure As she continued to work her way up to a crescendo. "You're a good girl Emma." I heard her say, but I still did not open my eyes as she finished huffing and planting.

However, I was disappointed, for I had always heard that you were supposed to experience some ultimate pleasure at the end of it all. As she withdrew, I felt her fall down beside me.

I opened my eyes, and beside me, once more, she was Mr. Phelker, and he lay there staring up at the ceiling, breathing heavily. I turned away and lay on my side, bringing my knees up to hug them. It hurt, and the feeling of guilt flowed through me. I closed my eyes again, and I don't know how long I lay there sobbing, but eventually, I fell asleep, and when I woke up, I was alone in the room. I sat myself up and sobbed some more before fumbling for my clothes. I dressed as quickly as possible and headed back to my quarters. I immediately stripped off again, stepped into the shower, and scrubbed the filth off me as I prayed for forgiveness. However, I soon learned that this had been what God had intended. But more on that later.

CHAPTER ELEVEN

— ❋ —

PLANS AND PRISONERS

The journey to the rendezvous in deep space would take several weeks. After Mr. Phelkar took her my calculations of the severe impact that would have on our resources, Major Plural decided to upload most of the crew. She only kept two marines downloaded; fortunately, one was me. This severely reduced my workload and meant I only went to work for about two hours a day, and I spent a lot of my time watching very old 24th-century movies set in the early days of solar colonialism. I admit I had a penchant for gushy old romance stories from those early days. I would lie in my bed with a big bowl of popcorn and a hot cup of cocoa and cry my eyes out over a corny love story.

I don't know why I had assumed that Major Plural would arrive in a blaze of glory and be hailed as the free American people's new leader because God does not work that way. He sends us challenges to make us better people and to curb our pride. So I shouldn't have been surprised when I heard her leadership was challenged. Actually, it was more than a surprise. I was absolutely livid. Although, of course, I never expressed it to anyone. I was delighted, but she chose me as part of her guard to attend a summit of captains on the USS Los Angeles.

I wore my dress uniform again for the first time since graduation. I felt proud as we waited to dock alongside the ship. Hardy and I walked directly behind her, and even Mr. Phelkar had to walk behind us until we were met by Captain Addison, commander of the Los Angeles and, if my opinion is worth anything, another sterling patriot.

The vessel was a top-of-the-line cruiser. We were led into a large briefing room where Major Plural took her place at the head of the table. She was wired up to a virtual reality device that would connect her to all the captains in the fleet while the rest of us watched on an overhead screen. The debate went on for a couple of hours.

There were some dissenters, and I made a mental note of their names and burned the recognition of their faces into my mind. This was where we separated the men from the boys and the women from the girls. Finally, Major Plural was asked to leave while the captains discussed which way they were going to go

As the major strode out, Hardy and I fell in behind her. An eternal wait began with Major Plural pacing back and forth, but I knew what the result would be, and yes, the majority backed her.

However, this was not the end of it. A couple of days later, I was summoned to a mission briefing with Major Plural, Addison, Tracker, and Hardy. I was punctual but also the last to arrive. They were standing over a large table with plans of the USS Constitution laid out.

Admiral Bailey, the head of the fleet before the surrender, had refused to recognize the majority decision, and I was to play my proud part in resolving that problem.

Major Plural glanced up at me as I entered the room. "Oh good, you're here. Grab yourself a coffee over there and come and join us." I didn't particularly want a coffee, but I took it as an order, poured myself one, and went to stand behind Hardy.

"Come around this side. You will see better. " Addison told me, and I went around. To my surprise, Addison stepped aside, leaving me a space between her and Major Plural my heart pounded being so close to her. It is an experience I recommend to any patriot that has the opportunity.

"So here is the situation. We need to get Helen Tracker on board the Constitution without detection so she can disable the computer systems. Stacey has shown us that there is a blind spot just here." Major Plural pointed to a rear airlock on the plans with a long well-manicured finger which I so desperately wanted to touch. We'll need you and Hardy to spacewalk her over there. When aboard, you are to get her to the central computer room. Here." The long perfect finger traveled across the floor plans to the room deep within the bowels of the ship. You shouldn't need to fight your way through, as we will have you dressed in the uniforms of techs serving aboard the Constitution. When Tracker has completed her business, you will remain there and protect her until we manage to board the ship ourselves. If successful, all power on board the ship will be out, so you need to gear up for night vision combat. Once we have taken the bridge, the pair of you will escort Helen to us. Pretty simple, huh?"

"Yes, ma'am."

"I sent these floor plans to your personal devices and room computers. Get familiar with this layout. You need to know it better than you do your own ship. " Addison advised us firmly. "The ship is vast and much bigger than it appears looking at just these plans. You can easily get lost if you don't know where you're going. "

"Yes, ma'am," Hardy responded.

I went ahead of Hardy as we headed out, but he came up behind me. "Hey, Dobson, wait up," he said aggressively, and I turned to face him. "You should know I strongly objected to a dumb rookie like you being on this mission. "

I was on a high from being in the presence of our leader, and I was not going to let this big ox berate me. "Of course, that is your prerogative, Sergeant."

"Don't be funny, Corporal." I hadn't intended to be. I thought I was more flippant than whimsical. "I don't know what you did to get all chummy with her, but it's my reputation on the line. I am this close to getting inside that bitch's knickers. No goddam rookie is gonna mess that up for me."

My high quickly left. How dare he speak of Major Plural in such a manner. "With all due respect, sarge. I don't believe that someone like the Major would be seen dead with the likes of you, but then I can't imagine any woman wanting to be."

He sneered contemptuously at me. "You don't know what you're talking about. You didn't see us at that party."

"No, I had better things to look at, but I did see the major after the party, and she certainly wasn't with you," I said contemptuously. "She is with Mr. Phelkar, a man more suited to her station."

Rather than get offended, Hardy laughed. "Then you must be the only one the doesn't know that the British shit is fucking Stacey Grant."

At that thought, I felt a small amount of vomit rise up into my throat and descend again. "Mr. Phelkar would not be so demeaning to himself to be seen with the likes of Lieutenant Grant."

Hardy screwed his face up in disgust at me. "You are such a weirdo, Dobson. Stacey Grant is no Jenna Plural, but she's still a nice piece of ass."

At that, I replied, "well, she's certainly more in your class, Sergeant. But make sure you check in with the clinic after making out with her."

He shook his head at me. "Watch yourself, Dobson, because I'll be watching you, and I'll make sure you're on a report if you so much as move your pinky finger in the wrong way on this mission."

"Oh, I show you, Sergeant Hardy. I watch everything." As he turned away and headed down the corridor, I shouted, "and the name is Dodgson, DODGSON."

Without looking back, he waved a dismissive hand at me. "Whatever."

As I turned away and headed back to the umbilical that connected the ship to the Liberty, I raised my eyes heavenwards. "Lord, will my work never be ended? Will the enemies of Major Plural Plural ever be vanquished?" I muttered in prayer.

When I returned to my quarters, I found a message waiting for me. A woman called Charlotte Kensett wanted to meet with me. No rank or title was given, and it was rather curious. I'm not sure how I would have responded under different circumstances; however, she informed me that she was contacting me under the authority of Major Plural, and I took her word on that. I called back over to her office on the USS Los Angeles, and I made an appointment for that afternoon.

When I went over there, it was all rather strange. Her offices had a number on the door but no indication of its purpose, such as a department name. I entered, and again it was odd for her office was pristine and un personalized. Her assistant greeted me personably and showed me to her office in the back.

Charlotte Kensett rose from her desk and greeted me. She was dressed in civilian clothes, a black colored shirt with a full black skirt to match. She was possibly around thirty. Despite not holding a military title rank or uniform, she bore herself in a very military fashion, standing quite upright as she rose to greet me. "Thank you for coming to see me at such short notice Corporal Dodgson. Please take a seat."

Saying nothing as I took the offered seat. She returned to her own and sat back. "I have been asked by the major to set up a new internal service to ensure security in the new situation we find ourselves in. Prior to this, I served as an agent for the Department of Outland security."

I was impressed Outland Security was a combined CIA and FBI division for all American off-world interests. American heroes in a clandestine world. However, something bothered me. "You do not sound American," I said coldly. Her accent was distinctly upper-class British.

A thin smile crossed her bright red lips. "Oh, I can assure you I am an American. Would you like to see my certificate of naturalization?" The offer, I am sure, was not a serious one.

"I am sure that is unnecessary, as Major Plural vouches for you," I replied.

"I am glad I have your approval, Corporal." She chuckled and sat back, studying me carefully. "Part of my responsibility is to assess everyone with regular access to her."

"That makes sense," I said. "There are many people who do not share her vision."

"Well, I'm glad I have your understanding." She picked up a pair of large black-framed glasses and, putting them on, glanced down at her screen and then back up at me. "I see there was an incident during your basic training. A recruit was murdered, and you were a suspect." She looked up at me again with a questioning look.

"Everyone was," I replied casually.

"Hmm, well, you were a little higher on that list than most. How do you explain that?"

"I was higher on the list because Randall and I did not get along."

Her eyes narrowed as she removed the glasses and leaned her elbows on her desk. "You don't sound too upset about the death of one of your colleagues in this manner."

"I'm not particularly." I shrugged. "He was a disgrace as a marine and a disgrace of a human being."

Kensett looked a little surprised by my response. "That is quite an unusual admission by a murder suspect. Usually, people would try to distance themselves from disagreements they've had with the victim."

"Isn't it the more suspicious to be dishonest? Randall was a pig. Should never have worn the uniform." I said, a little annoyed.

"Strong words." Her cold smile returned. "I take it you are a patriot, Corporal Dodgson?"

"And with all due respect, I consider it an insult even to be asked that question," I said curtly.

She shrugged that off. "My apologies. It is simply part of my job."

"Your job, as I understand it is to root out undesirable elements within the military and government, not cast aspirations upon dedicated members of the United States Marine Corps."

She tilted her head quizically. "Undesirable elements? Why'd you not simply use the word traitor?"

"They are not necessarily the same thing. A person is only a traitor after they have committed treason. Is it not best to remove a problem before it becomes a problem, Miss Kensett?"

Kensett now stared at me in deep concentration, and instead of answering my question, she said softly, "please do go on, Corporal Dodgson."

"Well, it is rather too late to do anything after the act of treason has been performed. We need to eliminate these threats before they become threats."

"What about their rights and due process?" She raised an eyebrow.

I stared at her. I could not help but wonder if she was the right person for intelligence. "Rights are for the innocent. Rights were never intended for traitors despite what the liberals say."

"Really? So what should we do if we find these undesirables?" She asked.

My suspicions about her intentions were heightened, but I spat at her in my agitation. "Eliminate them, Miss Kensett." I banged my fist on the table, yet she did not flinch. I was sure a slight smile was hidden amid those otherwise impassive features.

"Without a trial?" She chuckled and sat back, crossing her arms.

I stood up. "Forgive me, but I think this meeting is done. I do not know where you are going with this, and I no longer wish to participate."

"Emma!" She stood up, raising her hands defensively. "Do you mind me calling you Emma?"

I shrugged, "It's my name, and you are a civilian, so call me what you like."

She indicated the seat again. "Please sit back down, Emma. Just indulge me. But don't worry, whatever you say will not get you into trouble. To be honest, so far, I'm quite impressed."

I hesitated but eventually did as she asked, and we sat again. "Trials complicate things. All you end up with is some unpatriotic liberal lawyer coming along and talking about issues they had with their mommy and getting them acquitted."

Charlotte laughed at that, something I would find out that she rarely ever did. "So what do you propose we do with them." She smirked. Was she making fun of me?

"I feel like you're trying to manipulate me now, Miss Kensett. You know what is supposed to happen to these people. Why do you need me to say it?"

Kensett just sat staring at me until it became uncomfortable. "Call me Charlotte." She said, and another long silence passed until I made to stand up again, and she said quite calmly and seriously, "I think we can work together, Emma. You and I."

I scoffed at this, "I think, Miss Kensett, you are playing with me. I graduated at the bottom of my year. Barely. I am not stupid, but I'm not the stuff of the cloak-and-dagger world, and you know it. I am a marine, and I'm keeping it semper fi."

"Oh, I have no intention of asking you to step down from the marine corps." She stated firmly. "But I believe you have the potential to represent the interests of Jenna Plural on another level."

Now that piqued my interest. "Do go on?" I said, returning to my seat.

"Let me give you a scenario. You were present at the summit of the fleet captains. You saw several of them oppose the leadership of Major Plural." She started to swivel slowly back and forth in yer seat while toying with her glasses.

"Yes," I replied irritably. "It was disgraceful. I understand they have been removed from office pending investigations of potential ties with the enemy."

Charlotte stared at me for a moment. She dropped her glasses and said, "there is no evidence of collusion. Their only action has been to disagree with Jenna Plural."

I could see her studying my reaction to that. I gave her none. At least not in my expression. "Jenna Plural is our leader. I think anyone that stands in her way should be eliminated. It should be enough to be considered treason. It's all pretty simple. It's just there is no will to do what is necessary anymore."

"That is something Jenna intends to fix." I noted the informality with which she referred to the major. "And that's why I am in this position. We have arrested these officers, but they have not technically broken the law." She shrugged but kept her eyes fixed on my every reaction.

"Revolting against the rightful leader of our people is not a crime? " I shook my head, "if you're not willing to shoot them yourself, let me do it." It was an off-the-cuff remark, but I meant it.

Charlotte smiled through her thin lips. "Are you willing to prove that to me?"

"Miss Kensett, I met you for the first time less than thirty minutes ago. I do not believe I have anything to prove to you. My loyalty is to Major Plural and Major Plural alone."

"I'm trying to head up a team that will ensure the security of Major Plural. I answer to her and her alone, and she has given me a free hand to take whatever action is necessary to ensure the stability and security of her leadership. I want to make you part of that, unofficially."

"If this is aboveboard, why would you want to do it unofficially?" I scowled.

"You think Jenna Plural should soil her hands doing things that some fools will misinterpret or use in propaganda against her?" She said incredulously. "We must ensure the protection of those involved." She said it as if it should have been obvious to me. Plausible deniability, Emma."

"If it serves the best interests of Major Plural, then, of course, I am on board," I said.

"There's only one thing holding me back here, Emma. I need more than your word. I need some evidence that you mean what you say. And as part of that, I'd like to know your opinion on what I would do with the dissenting captains."

"Well, it would be much cheaper to use four bullets than four trials, and we can guarantee the outcome," I said.

"And how would I explain their deaths?" Kensett tilted her head questioningly again.

I shrugged. "Isn't that what you're paid to come up with?"

"Indeed it is." Kensett smiled. "However, are you willing to show me that you are more than words?"

"If that is necessary." I shrugged again.

"Come with me." She then led me out of the office and took me down two levels to the bowels of the ship. It was a small cargo area that clearly wasn't being used for cargo. Several locked storage containers were there, and an ununiformed guard was standing outside.

"Open one of them up," Kensett ordered.

The guard nodded and went to the nearest door. As he opened it, he shouted, "move to the center of the room! Kneel down! Hands behind your head!"

"Thank you, Mr. Jones. May I have your snap pistol and nightstick, please?" Charlotte asked, and without question or hesitation, he unfastened both from his belt holster and handed them over to her, and she led me into the makeshift cell.

A man, fairly elderly judging by his grey balding hair, knelt in the center of the room facing away from us. "This is former Captain Armitage of the USS San Diego. He is one of the commanders who wants us to surrender to the enemy. "

"The war is over." the commander said without turning around. "I just want to go home and see my family. My daughter graduates high school next month. We are tired of this war."

Charlotte smiled at me. "It makes my job easier when they give me a confession of that guilt." she then offered me the snap pistol, and I looked down at it. "Go ahead. You are authorized to deal with the situation."

I frowned, but I took the offered firearm. "Seriously?"

"Go ahead." She nodded toward the prisoner.

I raised the weapon and pointed it at the back of his head. I tried to squeeze the trigger, but I just couldn't do it. It made me feel sick. I looked at the gun. I looked at Kensett. "I can't do it."

Kensett looked most disappointed and gave a resigned sigh. "Fair enough, Emma. I thought we had something for a moment there. But it's all good." She reached out to take the gun from me.

I shook my head. "No, Charlotte, I don't think you understand." I turned to look at him with utter disgust. "I want to see his face. I want him to look at me when I do it. I want him to know what a patriot looks like. I want to be the last thing he sees. Just like Major Plural would."

"Oh my God, you're fucking insane." The captain said and made to get up. Kensett swiftly swung the nightstick into the back of his legs, then across his shoulders, sending him back down with a cry of pain. She turned back at me, pushed her glasses back up her nose, and nodded.

"Get up," I ordered, unable to hide the venom in my voice.

He did not move, and Kensett stepped over to him again and poked him in the back of the head with the nightstick. "You heard the lady. Move!"

He struggled to his feet, knowing he was not permitted to remove his hands from the back of his head. He turned around to face me, and there was fear in his eyes, the fear only a cowardly un-American traitor would have. This was not a godly man, and I stared at him for a moment enjoying the fact this traitor suffered God's wrath. I raised the weapon again, pointing at his face.

"Please don't, my daughter." He implored

"Maybe she will grow into a fine young lady now that you will no longer be an influence on her," I said softly and fired.

As his body fell to the floor, Charlotte turned to me with a wry smile. "Welcome to the team, Emma." She put out a hand for me to return the gun to her.

"Yes, yes, but what about the other three?" I said impatiently.

"Oh, you don't need to worry about that. I just wanted to see that you were willing to do what it took. "

"Oh, but I so wanted to." I sighed.

Charlotte raised an eyebrow. "I have another appointment soon. We will have to be quick."

I had a euphoric feeling for the rest of the night. Four traitors sent to hell by my own hand. It felt so good.

Chapter Twelve

Taking the Constitution

The call came through that all was prepared for the assault on the USS Constitution. I was halfway through a really good movie. I can't remember what it was now, but I remember being very disappointed that I wouldn't see the end. At least not that day. Hardy and Tracker were already there as I entered the bay where we were going to change into our emu suits and get ready to crossover to the enemy vessel.

"You're late," Hardy growled at me.

I found this rather curious statement. "No, I'm not, Sarge. A time wasn't specified other than to come now." He muttered something under his breath which I was sure was unpleasant as I saw Tracker give him a questioning frown.

Hardy had got the gear we needed ready. I pulled on the constitution replica uniform and then the emu suit over the top. I then slipped a snap pistol into the sleeve of the emu suit, and I turned to Helen to check the connections on her back, and she did the same to me. When Hardy turned his back to me, I pretended not to notice, and he said, "don't be childish, Dobson. Check my gear." I sighed and did as he said, pondering whether I should take this opportunity to loosen something, but the mission was more important, and he could wait.

"Do you two have a problem?" Tracker asked. "Because you're making me very nervous."

Hardy grunted in his usual manner, and I said, "no problem, Gunnery Sergeant. Sorry."

I have to say, despite his errant mouth, Hardy was good at what he did, and I trusted him as far as operations went. Not that that would ultimately redeem him from his inappropriate attention to Major Plural.

No! Judgment was going to come for Mr. Hardy, eventually, but for now, all that mattered was getting Tracker to that computer room. I could hear Helen breathing heavily over the internal communications, and I placed a hand upon her back to reassure her as the airlock slowly opened, and we looked out onto the blanket of space. She seemed to breathe heavier as we saw the Constitution, a mere speck of light at this moment, shining in the vastness of the expanse we had to cross.

Tracker did not have a jetpack. She did not need one and did not know how to use one even if she did. She had never done a spacewalk before, and she was not really doing one now since Hardy and I clipped tethers between ourselves and her. Then interlocking arms with her, we stepped out into the void powering up our packs as we went.

The trip across was uneventful. For most of it, we were too small to be picked up on the ship scanners. However, as we drew close, we had to go in via a very narrow vector that Stacey Grant had laid out. It was the best way to avoid detection by going through the Constitution's blind spot. They did not tell us prior to the mission about how outdated Grant's information was and the possibility of the flaw being fixed. Telling us could have added unnecessary tension, for we would have had to go anyway. However, her information proved solid, and we arrived at the assigned airlock, where several hours later, we tethered ourselves to the fuselage and waited. Airlocks are not designed to be opened in space from the outside. It can only be done when a ship is in docking mode. We had to wait for whatever agents the Major and Kensett had arranged for us. A full ten minutes passed, and looking down on the air supply, I saw we were rapidly running out of time as the dial reached the halfway mark. Should it go over, there would be no way to return to the USS Los Angeles in time.

"Okay, that's it. Abort the mission." Hardy stated frustratedly.

"We can wait a bit longer," I said.

"That's not your call, Marine." Hardy snapped.

"No, but it is mine." Said Tracker firmly. "Everything rides on this mission. If we fail, we may as well turn ourselves over to the Peons."

"With all due respect Gunnery Sergeant, I think that would be better than being dead." Hardy sneered.

If I had any doubts about the low levels that Hardy would sink to, I certainly didn't now. Dying for one's country is the noblest form of death.

"I understand your concern Sergeant Hardy, and I'm sorry, but we will wait." Tracker said firmly. "The agents on the other side are personally handpicked by Charlotte Kensett, and trust me, I know exactly how good she is."

The only response from Hardy was an irritated sigh. A few minutes later, I looked down at my gauge again, and it was definite. Should we attempt to return to the Los Angeles, we would run out of air about seven minutes before arriving. I don't know anyone who could hold their breath for seven minutes. Our fate was sealed. We either entered the Constitution, or they picked up our corpses hanging outside.

When the airlock suddenly sank into the fuselage a few minutes later and slid aside, we all breathed a sigh of relief that we could breathe a sigh of relief. We first pushed Helen in before detaching from the bulkhead and following her. The door closed behind us, and we detached ourselves from Helen as air filled the room and gravity was restored. We removed the EMU suits, which we unceremoniously dumped on the floor. Then the internal door opened, and we stepped inside the Constitution. We never got to see the individual who had let us in. They had done it remotely from another location. Once the inner airlock closed behind us, we casually strolled down the corridor, chatting aimlessly, passing other crewmen who were unaware of our intentions.

We turned down the right corridors as if they were familiar, for Hardy and I had memorized the directions. When we crossed the threshold of the restricted area, we knew it wouldn't be that easy anymore. As we turned another corner, a crewman approached and asked us to show him our authorization for being in the area. Of course, we had no such documentation, so I stepped up to him and quickly pulled my snap pistol out of my belt as if reaching into my back pocket. I thrust into his stomach and fired as Hardy stepped behind him and covered his mouth to avoid any potential screams or calls for help.

I admit that I do feel guilty for this particular demise, for I do not know whether he would have been loyal to Major Plural or not. It turned out in the end that most of the crew were patriots. I re-holstered my weapon as the man expired. Hardy then lifted him over his shoulder and said, "keep going. I will find somewhere to stash this guy so he won't be found for a while."

So alone, Tracker and I continued and eventually found the computer room. The security was simple. Someone was always inside, and it could only be opened from inside. That, of course, is if you don't have a Helen Tracker. She pulled out a device, slapped it on the lock, pressed a few buttons, and it made an irritating buzzing noise until it finally beeped, and the door slid open. I stepped in and shot the first startled tech in the face and then fired at the second. I cursed myself as I missed, giving them time to duck down behind a console. I went to fire again, but Tracker grabbed my arm. "Be careful you don't hit the computer."

I stepped around the counter where the last tech was crawling on the floor and put him out of my misery with another single shot. Tracker was already tapping into the keyboard. "Damn it to hell!" Tracker exclaimed. "They have added an additional firewall which I did not antici-pate." Her fingers darted over the keyboard faster than I'd ever seen anyone type. "Every time I look like I'm going to bring it down, the code rewrites itself and buries itself deeper into other code. It's actually quite beautiful if I was on the other side of this."

I spun around as the door opened, aiming my gun. I lowered it just as fast when I saw it was Hardy. He turned around and reached out the door to grab Tracker's device and bring it inside before the door closed. Now we were in control of who left and who came in.

"How is it going?" he asked.

"She is having problems," I said. "Something about code and stuff."

He turned to Tracker. "Can you do it or not?"

"Maybe, but it will be easier if you shut up and leave me alone."

He turned away and muttered, "dumb bitch," and even Tracker stopped what she was doing to look up and glare at him for a second.

"Okay, I'm in, but I don't know how long I can hold back the algorithm for the firewall, but it's rewriting its code again."

Hardy and I pulled on our night vision glasses as she started typing again. It was quite a bizarre sensation when everything went out. You get so used to the hum and vibration of a ship that you don't feel or hear it but be-come instantly aware when it's no longer there. Slowly the ship died, and the lights went out last of all. Hardy and I switched on our emergency lights attached to our night vision glasses which we had not yet activated. Silhouetted in the dim light, Helen told us, "I don't know how long this is going to stay down for. It could come up at any time. This firewall is state-of-the-art. I'm going to have to stay here and constantly monitor it."

"That's not part of the plan, Sergeant," Hardy said.

"There is no other option," she snapped back at him.

"Yes, there is." He slipped a limpet mine from his belt, slapped it on the computer, and pressed the button before we could say anything. There was a fifteen-second delay, and we ran out the door and dove to the floor as it exploded. Tracker was positively livid as she rose to her feet. "Hardy, you are a dumb ass. We are now never going to get the ship online again."

With snap pistols out, we turned off the flashlights, turned on the light intensifiers, and slowly made our way toward the bridge. We started hearing the dull thuds on the outside of the walls. The sound of troop pods launched from the Los Angeles, hitting the hull. Normally they would blow their way in, but we wanted the ship intact, so they made their way to the airlocks.

. While the crew panicked, the USS Los Angeles marines took control of the Constitution without firing another shot. I would learn later that the major herself came on board and personally took command from Admiral Baines. He would officially announce his resignation, and we never heard from him again.

I became part of the emergency team thanks to Hardy's screw-up. We had to set up emergency lighting in the ship's key areas, and Helen and her team managed to get some operational life support working. We did not have the resources to transfer the crew while we worked out how to get the ship back up and running.

Mr. Phelkar transferred over to the Constitution, as did most of the senior crew from the Lewis Puller. I returned to aiding Mr. Phelkar and reviewed the records that had been sent to us of supplies and equipment. We had a stroke of luck. One of the US vessels had been transporting a computer system similar to the Constitution for an upgrade for another ship. As soon as I informed Helen Tracker, she commandeered it via Captain Addison. Major Plural officially transferred her command to the Constitution, and Addison came with her as her first officer. I worked closely with her as she often liaised with Mr. Phelkar on the supply and crew issues. Several days later, Tracker restored most of the internal power, but the engines and defense systems were still offline.

Chapter Thirteen

Dead Reckoning

When things started to develop some semblance of order, I actually got an evening off duty and ventured out to a mess hall. These were more like nightclubs and bars on this vast ship. As I entered the bar, I found Mr. Phelkar sitting alone on a comfy-looking couch, nursing a beer and deep in thought.

"Hey there, Mr. Phelkar." He looked startled as he looked up at me with those beautiful brown eyes. This quickly changed to his usual warm smile. "Mind if I join you?" I asked.

"I will be delighted by your company." He replied, sitting up and indicating the armchair chair opposite him.

"Thank you, Sir," I replied. As I sat down, he waved to one of the stewards.

"You know, I'm not an officer." He chuckled. "You don't have to call me 'Sir.' You don't even have to call me Mr. Phelkar. My name is Michael."

"What sort of a name is Phelkar?" Stacey Grant suddenly appeared, jumped over the couch's back, and landed next to him. He gave me an apologetic smile and rolled his eyes, clearly annoyed that the Jezebel had interrupted our private moment. "I mean, it's not like it's even a real name."

"It was a tradition back when Martian independence was a thing. People started making up names that had no national boundaries. My name would have been Phillips had my parents been born on Earth. That was before the war, and both sides decided that discussing independence for Mars was treason."

Stacey looked utterly bored as he spoke and very rudely yawned before looking at me. "Phelks is an okay bloke, but he can sometimes be such a long-winded wanker."

I tried to smile back. "Yes, Ma'am," I said curtly.

The stupid Australian did not seem to pick up on the fact that Mr. Phelkar nor I wanted her here. "We are off duty. Cut the Ma'am shit and call me Stacey. Actually, cut the Ma'am shit altogether. I don't go in for that."

No respect for the chain of command. I did not find that surprising. Australians are not exactly cultured or well-educated. "Yes, ma... Stacey."

"Seriously, Dodgson. Tonight, we leave the war behind us." She smiled, not that cheeky smile she perpetually wore, but a more sincere one.

I smiled coldly, "Then please call me Emma." I said sarcastically.

Stacey grinned her stupid grin, "How about I call you Em and make it more Aussie-like?"

Oh, my sweet God! She was as dumb as poop, but I just laughed it off. "As you wish."

"I have worked with you a while now, but I don't know much about you," Mr. Phelkar asked me. "Why did you join the Marines?"

"Bloody hell, Phelks," Stacey interrupted rudely. "You have two of the hottest women in the damn fleet sitting here, and you wanna talk shop!" She winked at me. I chuckled lightly, embarrassed for her.

Stacey ordered some shots for us before turning back to me. "So, how come a cute girl like you is all alone?"

"Well, I wasn't alone." I snapped back but flushed slightly when Mr. Phelkar winked at me seductively.

I know Mr. Phelkar never talked about our relationship in his book, but that just shows what a true gentleman he is. He knows we could never be together, for Major Plural had taken him as her own, and that is her right. However, I am not ashamed of it, for you will see, as I conclude this story, it was ordained to be what it was.

Stacey grinned and, without any semblance of manners, said, "I'm sorry. Did I interrupt something? You know, I always thought you preferred girls."

Dodgson glared at her in disgust. "What have I ever done to give you that idea?"

She shrugged. "You remind me of a friend of mine. My best mate, actually. She liked the ladies."

Mr. Phelkar came to my rescue. He is such a darling man. "You must be worried about her with everything going on."

Stacey went on about some dead friend of hers, but I wasn't listening to her boring story as the steward returned with our shots. I usually don't imbibe hard liquor, but the Australian slut had made me *so* mad.

"Same again, and keep them coming." Mr. Phelkar instructed as he took his.

"Nice one, let's call this a party." Stacey grinned.

Oh my gosh, that was it for me. "Actually, I should probably go," I said.

Stacey looked over at me. "I'm sorry, mate. I have made you uncomfortable. I didn't mean to. Please stay."

"Stacey's mouth is more active than her brain," Mr. Phelkar grinned at me but had that "please don't leave me alone with this insane woman look upon his face, and for his sake, I stayed.

"Ain't that the truth." Stacey smiled. "You're quite a cute girl," she said appreciatively.

Oh gross! However, the Melbourne Firebomb drink was going to my head fast, and I giggled. "I'm *really* not into women."

Stacey shrugged. "Nor am I. At least, I wasn't until I met Jenna Plural. Now she *is* hot."

That was something we could agree on. "Now that, I cannot deny."

"You cannot help but wonder what she's like in bed with all that genetic perfection." Stacey downed her third firebomb.

"I don't think that's an appropriate way to talk about our commanding officer," Mr. Phelkar said. Of course, he was absolutely right.

"More inappropriate than rooting her, Phelks?" Stacey grinned.

"What are you talking about?" Mr. Phelkar, again the perfect guy, jumped to the defense of Major Plural's honor.

Stacey grinned at him. "Rumor has it that you're fucking the major."

"I don't know what you're talking about." He insisted.

"Looks like we are both outmatched when it comes to gaining the affection of Mr. Phelkar," The hussy said to me with a chuckle.

My head was swimming as by now I'd drank my third shot. "Well, it certainly increases the challenge." The firebombs were taking effect, and I found myself saying things I otherwise wouldn't.

"Well, he knows what he is missing with me." Stacey grinned, glancing up at me.

After downing another firebomb, I glared at Stacey. "Is there anyone that Mr. Phelkar isn't sleeping with?" I was again being sarcastic, but it went straight over pea brain's head.

"Well, it's not like he's an amazing stud or anything, but there was an amazing lack of men on the Chesty."

"Well, thank you," He snapped at her.

She just laughed. "Oh, come on, Phelks, I'm just joshing you, ya moron." She slipped her arm into his. "So, you and the boss. That's just a rumor?"

"Of course it is," He stated firmly.

Stacey looked over at me. "So, what do you think of a young Emma here? She's quite a cutie."

"She's younger than my daughter."

"I like older men," I replied without thinking, the devil's liquor now having a hold.

Stacey glared at Mr. Phelkar. "How old do you think I am?"

"Never thought about it, to be honest. How old are you?"

"I'm twenty-seven." She then looked at me. "How old are you?"

"I'm nineteen."

I grinned and shrugged. "And my daughter is twenty-two, so I stand by my statement."

"You're such a fucking arsehole." Stacey pouted.

We drank some more, and I saw Mr. Phelkar staring at me lustfully. If he wanted me again, he could have me, and I let him know by returning the look. However, he said, "as nice as this has been, I think I'm going to retire. I have to be up early in the morning."

"You see, Em, that's the problem with older guys. They may know what they're doing in the bedroom but have no stamina."

I laughed and found myself saying, "it's the knowing what they are doing that makes them most interesting."

"And on that note, I will bid you ladies goodnight."

"Yeah, yeah, fuck you, mate." Stacey grinned at me.

She watched Phelkar go with a look of deep concentration. She then looked back at me. "Sorry mate, but I'm hornier than a jumbuck in the mating season, and I think he is too." She jumped out of her seat. "Catch you later, Em." I watched her leave with disgust on my face.

Surely Mr. Phelkar would not demean himself with that potentially pox-ridden whore.

They say that curiosity killed the cat, but I didn't care since I hate cats. As she reached the door, I got up and followed her from a discreet distance. She stopped outside Mr. Phelkar's cabin, and I had to duck around the corner as she turned back toward me. Fortunately, she was so wrapped up in her evil plans that she did not notice me. When I looked back around the corner, she was pacing up and down. She stopped and reached into her pocket, pulled out a small bottle of pills, popped one into her mouth, and then continued pacing again. A couple of minutes later, she knocked on the door. Mr. Phelkar opened it, and they stood talking for a moment, although I couldn't hear them. To my utter horror and disgust, he leaned in and kissed her quite passionately. Poor Mr. Phelkar. He made to pull her into the room, but instead, she pulled him out, and they turned in my direction. I disappeared back down the corridor and returned to the mess hall. You have to understand that it was not his fault. Men are weak, and it is hard for them to resist the temptations of a woman. Especially a brazen hussy like Stacey Grant. It is the woman's responsibility to ensure she does not arouse him. At least, that is what my father always told me when he came to my room at night.

I headed toward the bar, and as I ordered my drink, I did not realize I was standing next to Helen Tracker until she spoke to me. "Hey Em, how's it going."

I turned and looked at her, I don't know if it was the drink, but she appeared more attractive than usual. Her flame-red hair hung around her shoulders rather than tired up as normal. "Hey, Sarge. Well, it was going well until that Australian showed up."

"Who, Stacey? She's pretty cool once you get to know her." She laughed. "But it's not easy to get to know her. Despite her behavior, she is pretty tight-lipped about herself."

I just harrumphed and paid for my beer. Tracker looked around, then back at me. "Well, you're alone, and I'm alone. You up for some company?" she asked.

I smiled at her. "Sure, why not?" As I'm sure you are aware from reading this, I'm not the world's most sociable person, but it turns out I become one when intoxicated. For some reason, I did not want to return to the booth where I'd been sitting with Mr. Phelkar and the Jezebel, and we found a quiet secluded corner.

We chatted away about anything but work. She told me about growing up in New York, and I told her about my life in Arizona, excluding the parts involving my father. We did discover a common passion for old movies, and when the barman called for last orders, she suggested we go back to her place and watch one.

Oh, if only I had listened to my inner wisdom and said no. If only I had not got drunk. If only, and then some. Things would have been a whole lot different.

The one difference between Helen and me was that she was a lot messier than me. Not exactly dirty, just untidy. She seemed to bring work home with her, and pieces of old tech were lying around everywhere. The couple of chairs she had were piled high with chip boards and spare parts.

"oh, don't worry bout that. We can just sit on the bed."
She laughed at the look on my face as I stared at the mess.

As I stared at her large widescreen television, I asked,
"how come you have this and I don't?" I pouted.

She looked a little embarrassed as she said, "think of it
as an engineer's indulgence. One of the first things I wired
up was my TV. It's not considered an essential service, so I
couldn't do it for everybody, but I'll see what I can do for
you tomorrow."

She heated some nachos with some melted cheese. Basic
cooking facilities in our quarters were something we did
not have before coming to the Constitution.

She then jumped onto her bed, scooted over to the
side by the wall then patted the place beside her. "Come
on," she said, but I hesitated momentarily. "I'm not going
to bite you. Well, not unless you ask me to." I took the
last statement as an innocent joke. I laughed lightly and
climbed onto the bed beside her.

We didn't watch an old movie in the end. Instead, we
put on a modern comedy that came out just before the fall
of the US. I could not help but wonder what happened to
the famous actors and actresses that were in the film, but
it was funny, and we laughed a lot. Toward the end, with
the nachos finished and the plate tossed aside, I felt Helen's
hand upon mine, and looking down, I saw she was holding
it. My eyes moved up to look at hers, and she was looking
into mine as she bit her lower lip. She moved toward me,
I moved toward her, and we kissed. She ran her hands up
me. I found myself pulling her close against my body. I
know what you're thinking, but no, I am not going to go

into detail about what happened that night. While Mr. Phelkar and Captain Grant may well be willing to discuss their lewd acts together, I am not so willing. I'm not here for your voyeuristic entertainment. I will say how much of an amazing experience it was. Helen was so much more giving and gentle, and there was a whole lot less grunting.

However, when I woke up the next morning, I felt dirty and ashamed, and I slipped out of that bed and left Helen asleep, snoring lightly. I dressed quickly, hurried back to my room, took a long shower, and spent a long time praying in penance. Since that day, I have not permitted alcohol to pass my lips other than in Holy Communion.

News of the incoming French fleet reached us, and everything became a hustle and a bustle. The pressure was on Helen to get the computer up and running and bring the USS Constitution online. I was placed on the defensive line. My role was to join the team, stopping anyone who managed to board the Constitution. It would not be easy, considering we still had limited lighting, no internal defense systems, and the ship couldn't move, making it easier for Peon troops to land on the outside and blow their way in. However, as was the nature of the battle in space, there were never any surprises, and we could see who was coming from all directions. The Major had the option to get her faster ships out of there, but that would mean abandoning the Constitution and some of the civilian ships that had started to join the flotilla.

One of the things someone in my rank found frustrating was not knowing the details of the battle plan. I was mightily miffed when I heard that a group of ships under the command of Captain Addison had taken off. I had no idea this was part of the major's plan, and I doubted my judgment of character, for I personally found Addison to be a sterling individual.

I was teamed up with Malcolm Hardy again. While I was not overly pleased with that, at least it was someone I knew how to work with. He may have been a pig of a man, but he was a great marine. However, I was pleased to be issued the new Glock penetrators. They were an upgrade from our usual snap pistols, carrying a larger round at a much faster velocity. We were also issued Ruger P7 assault rifles since the chance of a hole penetration on the Constitution was negligible. Our communicators were switched only to pick up status reports and orders. I could not even communicate with Hardy and would need to work with hand signals when silence was necessary.

We were near the bow of the ship when the attack came. Unbeknownst to me, the battle raged for a couple of hours before anyone got near the Constitution. Major Plural had done everything she could to protect the flagship, her most powerful weapon. However, there was no doubt some would get through as this was a primary target, and it would be even more so once they found it just hung in space, not even able to launch the hundreds of fighters of the Air Force.

When the attack came, it was strange because we could barely hear the thud thud thud of troop capsules landing up on the outside. The hull was so thick with Murcuranium. It amused me when I later learned that the initial attempts to blast through backfired because they used insufficient explosives to get through the hull and fire balls blew back into the capsules, killing those who had started the attack. How funny!

They quickly adapted and began manually burning their way through the bulkheads with torches. It was not a particularly productive move because we literally stood in front of where they were burning through and opened fire into the capsules as soon as they opened up. However, the sheer quantity thrown at us eventually became overwhelming, and Peons started getting through onto the ship.

It appeared at first that we would lose as we started to be forced out of the outer corridors losing many troops in the process. We kept up the fire as more and more men filled the corridors. As more and more of our people started shouting, "I'm out," referring to their ammo, Hardy called for a retreat. We went further into the ship, away from the bulkheads.

I don't know how many we killed that day. I was mowing them down with delight. Yet more were constantly coming in. I know the final count is estimated that they lost three times what we did. As things started to seem lost, Tracker managed to bring one of the defenses online and electrified the outer hull. Anyone who was outside the ship fried instantly like bacon in a pan. It also meant no more troops could land. However, that did not mean a certain victory, for should they take the bridge, they could disable Tracker's work or do what Hardy did and blow up the computer room again. However, with Hardy and me out of ammo, we could do nothing but hunker down in one of the rooms and hope more supplies could be got to us.

With no ammo in or rifles, Hardy and I went to ground. We were in some officer's cabin, and after radioing in our location and situation, we learned that the Los Angeles had managed to get more troops on board on the opposite side of the ship.

For us, though, with no ammo, the battle was over for the time being. We stood back, out of sight of the door, so we could hear someone enter before they saw us.

I don't recall how the subject came up, but as we sat and talked, Hardy found himself saying, with considerable irritation, "I can't believe she is fucking that English loser."

"She is our leader." I shrugged. "Who she chooses to make love with is entirely her own concern. She deserves whoever she chooses to have."

Hardly looked at me and laughed, "Make love? You are a strange little bird, Dobson. Why on Earth Jenna made you a corporal, I will never understand. You really don't have what it takes to be a marine."

I was already annoyed at him, and this only aggravated me more. "Because I choose not to use profanity that makes me less of a marine?"

"Your sycophantic defense of that pathetic Englishman is what makes you less of a marine, Dobson." He snorted.

"Mr. Phelkar is a gentleman and a fine man," I said with irritation.

"Not while he's fucking my girl. Something has to be done about him, and I promise you, little girl, I will remove him from the picture somehow."

"I think it is disrespectful to speak about the major that way." I was sure that I was reddening in my anger. "And she is not your girl."

He grinned. "Not yet, Dobson, but she will be. I can promise you that." A filthy grin crossed his smug face. "And then I will part those sweet cheeks and have my way. Ooh, wee!" He laughed.

It took me a moment to realize he was not talking about her face, and that's when I got my sign. It was now or never. I had to take him out and dispatch him to hell.

CHAPTER FOURTEEN

BIRTH OF THE CONFEDERATION

As he turned away, I reached up behind him. I brought my arm around his throat and my knee into his back, pulling him toward me. It was foolish, for he swung forward and threw me over the top of his head with sheer brute force. I landed flat on the floor in front of him, and as I looked up, I stared into his handgun barrel. "What the fuck do you think you're doing, girl?"

"My duty, Sergeant." He was so confused that he was not paying that much attention. I swung my arm up, knocking the gun aside, and with my other fist clenched tightly, I punched him right up into the groin. He let out a cry and took a step back. It was just enough for me to get back on my feet. I swung a kick at his wrist, and he dropped the gun as I reached for the blade attached to my thigh. But he had recovered and came at me, slamming me against the wall and winding me. My knee came up into his groin as I headbutted him. His grip loosened, and I tried to shove him back. But his forehead slammed into my face, my head hit against the wall hard, and blood flowed from my lip as it cut into my teeth. I believed at that point that I would not win this fight. All the tactics in the world did not make up for this brute force of the giant man against the skinny girl from Sedona.

He still looked bewildered by what was going on, but as I withdrew my blade, he punched me again, and it fell with a clatter to the floor as I hit the wall again. He made to grab his gun, but as he leaned over, I slammed a knee into his stomach. It was almost a farce as we both tried to get weapons to no avail. It's kinda funny looking back at it now. Alas, this time, I had only hit his body armor, and he was barely fazed as he pulled up his rifle.

I then took a hail mary act and, leaping into the air, I wrapped my arms around his neck and my legs around his waist, bringing him down with the sheer force of my forward momentum. He landed back down on the ground with me sitting on his chest. I knew I could not hold him for long, for his arms were not trapped, and I punched, and I punched, and I punched the heck out of him. I hit him in the face every time he tried to push me off, but I resisted with sheer determination and God's will and continued to punch his ugly, sinful face until it became a bloody pulp.

His body grew weaker under me, and his arms fell to his sides. I slipped my hands around the thickly muscled neck. It was so large I could barely get a grip around it, and he suddenly threw me back with a sudden burst of energy, and I landed on my rear end between his legs.

He sat up, but I breathed a sigh of relief as I could see he was blinded by the amount of blood in his eyes. I bought my knee up to my chest and slammed the heel of my boot into his groin. He rolled over in the fetal position, crying in agony. I got to my feet. I looked around the room. Grabbing a bedside lamp, I yanked it out of the socket and placed it on the floor. I put my foot on it and pulled the cable out of its connections.

Hardy was trying to get up, so I gave him several hard whacks with the table lamp across the side of the head until he lay groaning and barely moving. I tide the wire into a lasso. I placed it over his head and lifted his head by the hair to get it around his neck. I then placed my foot on his head and pulled with all my might so that it tightened. He seemed to recover slightly once more and grabbed at his neck, unable to make a noise or even breathe. But I knew it was over for him then and there. I pulled harder, bent down, pulled his head up once more, and wrapped it several times around his neck as his struggles weakened.

I stood watching in fascination and a little excitement as this heathen servant of evil started to turn blue. I was even a little disappointed when his bulging blood soaked eyes rolled up into his head, and he stopped moving. I sighed and got down on one knee to feel for a pulse. He was most definitely dead. However, I wanted to make absolutely sure. So I placed my foot upon his neck, grabbed his hair, and pulled hard until I heard the crack of his vertebrae.

I slumped into a chair to catch my breath. I laughed lightly, quite proud of myself. No one was going to disrespect my leader. I then removed the cable from his neck and dropped it into the garbage chute to ensure my DNA was not on the method of his death. Not that there was likely to be an autopsy. Malcolm Hardy would just be one of the many dead that day.

I carefully re-entered the corridor making sure it was clear. I had to put some distance between myself and Hardy's body. However, I'd be a witness to his death, and the fact that I survived with no dead Peons around him could cause suspicion. Not that I had done anything wrong, but others may not see it that way.

Fortunately, the fighting had moved on, and it was relatively calm until suddenly, the ship shook and shuddered, and I seriously thought we were about to break up. I sat down and covered my head with my hands in the normal emergency procedure, but everything went calm except for the occasional thud against the hull.

I did not know it at the time, but we had just got caught in the wake of the collision between the Lady Liberty as Stacey Grant took out a Peon cruiser with a head-on collision, and the dull thuds that followed were parts of those ship hitting us as they broke up.

I had no idea where I was, and as things settled, I looked up with trepidation before getting up again. I decided to continue heading on toward the bridge. I stopped when I heard German voices ahead of me, but I knew it was game over for the Peons when the mini guns dropped out of the ceiling.

I quickly checked the transponder pin that I made sure I had this time. It was blinking away, letting the automated sensors know I was not a target. The distant sound of the machine guns firing showed me how far the enemy was from me. When they stopped firing, I continued on. When

I arrived, I saw Major Plural had boarded the ship during the combat, and my pride in her swelled. She had put herself in harm's way and did not hide like many leaders when her people were fighting.

As she stood on that bridge giving orders, the sun appeared on the screen. A distant shining globe, causing her to become a silhouette with a golden hue about her. I wish I could have captured that moment in a photograph, but it will be forever imprinted in my mind.

She looked at me with concern at my bloodied and bruised state. "Are you okay?" She asked.

I nodded, "Was good to get some payback after what happened on the Chesty," I grinned. Of course, I was referring to all the times Hardy had harassed her.

The new Admiral gave me a wide smile. "Amen, sister," she said. "Now go wash up and get that face seen too, corporal."

"Yes, Ma'am,"

As she turned to leave, she asked, "where is Sergeant Hardy?"

I looked back sadly, "I'm sorry major. He didn't make it. I..."

Major Plural sighed. "That's war for you, Corporal. Don't let it get to you, and don't forget it, either. And change into a uniform more fitting to your new commission, Lieutenant Dodgson."

I could not help but grin when she said that, but I finally noticed Mr. Phelkar smiling broadly. It was not until I read his book Jenna Plural Wants You that I realized how pleased he was with my work dispatching Hardy.

I noticed Helen look over at me and smile. I smiled back and hurried from the bridge.

It became known as The Battle of Deep Space, and victory was ours while we took heavy casualties. We lost several ships, including the Lady Liberty and the Lewis Puller. I was surprised when no one ever asked anything about Malcolm Hardy. He appeared on casualty lists a few days later, and a few days after that, he appeared on the mass funeral ledgers as having been ejected into space. The time-honored tradition for the dead since man first ventured out among the planets.

Crews started receiving new orders as, once more, transfers were needed to fill vacant positions across the flotilla. I started to become concerned when I did not receive my orders. It was like I'd been forgotten. However, I eventually received a call to visit with Captain Addison. Or rather, Commodore Addison now. I went to her office by the bridge. I was curious to see they were setting up television cameras in the center of the Constitution's vast control center. Apparently, there was going to be some sort of broadcast, but I quickly went in to see Admiral Plural's number two.

I was surprised to see her dressed in civilian clothes. It was the first thing she spoke to me about. "Ah, Dodgson! Come on in and take a seat. We can skip the formalities here," she said as I made to stand to attention and salute. I took the seat but sat upright professionally as she slipped back behind her desk. "Forgive my appearance, Dodgson. We are changing our uniforms for reasons that will become clear later. I do, however, have an urgent issue to discuss with you. As you are aware, our victory came at quite a cost in personnel. We have lost many officers. We have been making a short list of enlisted personnel we hope to commission to fill those roles. The major was most insistent that we include your name on that list. Is that something you would entertain?" Addison asked.

"I am honored to serve her in whatever way she sees fit," I said honestly.

"We want you to form a specialist unit willing to take on hazardous recon missions. We'll need you to go to areas we plan to attack and return with the information for our planning. I will not lie. It is highly dangerous as you and a few personnel will be sent behind enemy lines. Are you up to that, Dodgson?"

"Of course, ma'am, I am a marine."

Addison smiled. "We will make the post official in a few days. In the meantime, please do not speak about it. There is going to be a special announcement by the Admiral today. Make sure you watch it and understand it. If you have any problems with it, come and see me. If you disagree with its content, there will be no repercussions, but it will affect you receiving the commission."

I left her office most curious about what Major Plural was going to announce. When I returned to my quarters, I found Helen waiting for me. "Hey Emma, can we talk?"

"I guess so," I said, opening my door and letting her in. This was going to be awkward. "Want a coffee?"

"Might as well while we still can. I heard they're going to start rationing." She said as she sat down. I didn't respond to this as I wasn't paying attention to what she said. As I made the drinks, she continued to speak to me. I handed her the drink, and she looked at the concern on my face. "What is wrong?" she asked gently.

"I don't know if you have any ideas of where we are going or if this is going anywhere at all." My voice was nervous and uneasy as I blurted it out. "You and me, I mean."

She sighed, took my cup from my hand, then placed both on the table beside her. She took my hands in hers and said softly, "they are giving me a commission, Emma, and that means anything between us will be fraternization."

I did not say anything. My mind was trying to register everything that was going on. Part of my brain had locked away my encounter with Helen. I was desperately attracted to her, which conflicted with everything I understood as a servant of God. Same-gender relationships may have been mainstream for hundreds of years, but not for people like me. However, it just felt so right, and while I thought the devil was testing me, I knew the devil could not make me happy like I was with Helen Tracker. My face must have been expressionless. She looked so nervous. "Please say something, Emma. "

She looked startled as I sat down and pulled her onto my lap, my arm around her, looking down into that pale, brightly freckled, beautiful face. "I'm not supposed to say anything." I whispered, "they have given me a commission too. So it won't be fraternization." Her eyes lit up, and that gave me such joy. I laughed lightly, and before she could say anything, I leaned in to kiss her. Before anything else could be said or done, my TV screen came on as it does with any emergency broadcast. We both looked up and saw the bridge of the Constitution.

The doors opened, and Major Plural entered, looking resplendent in a black nondescript dress uniform with no national insignia. She strode purposely forward, knowing she was already on the camera. All around, the seated crew stood up to attention. As she stopped in front of the camera, she raised her hand to indicate that they should sit and then looked ahead. She paused and looked around at her crew before looking back at the camera and speaking.

"I pray that I come to you today as a beacon of hope. I have assumed command of the loyal remnants of the allied forces. You should have already heard about the great victory over the Europeans in the Battle of Deep Space. We emerged from it stronger and more committed to the cause of freedom than ever before, for I say to you now, as clear as I can be." Her voice rose aggressively, and she slammed a leather-gloved fist on the podium. Anger and passion were vehement in her eyes. "We completely and utterly reject the surrender of the leaders of the Pacific Alliance. We won't roll over like a dog under the tyranny of the European Union. We won't hide. We won't run. We won't capitulate. We did not ask for this war." Spittle flew from her mouth. "I did not ask to sacrifice the lives of our young. I don't love war." She paused then shouted, "I love freedom, and I will fight, bleed, and die to see that restored." Her voice lowered, "It is not going to be easy. You are bloodied and bruised, but we have shown the Europeans that we will be masters of our destiny. I say to you all," She raised a clenched fist and shouted once more.

"Rise up. Rise up and be counted as a hero. Rise up and turn on your oppressors. We will be out here, growing in number every day. Taking the fight wherever a European cowers and hides. We are battered, but we are unbroken. We will strike at the very heart of European domination. We will destroy every ship. We will destroy every base. We will destroy every European we encounter until no more Europeans are left. We will take no prisoners. We will pursue the enemy with our hearts filled with vengeance for the loved ones we have left behind on Earth. I dedicate myself, and I ask you to do the same, to the total eradication of the European Union. I don't bring you victory today, but I do bring you the promise of victory tomorrow. It may take months. It may even take years. I promise you, with everything that I am. And to you Peon scum out there. I am coming for you. The day will arrive when the European Union is no more than a footnote in the history books. This is total war, and we are coming home."

"She's done it." Helen looked at the screen with amazement before looking up at me, "Emma, what is wrong?"

Tears were streaming down my face, although I made no sound. I just looked down at her, "I'm so proud to be part of this, Helen. Aren't you just so proud of her? The major, I mean. "

She did not respond at first, and her face was quite passive, but then she smiled, "I have worked with Jenna for several years, and when you've seen her in ways that I have.... Well, you see the reality beyond the legend. I have seen her at her highest and her lowest." She sighed. "I wish I could see her with your eyes, but I can't. She's a friend, and I can't step back and see her as this woman who is the great Commander in Chief."

"Yet she is." I smiled, and as she climbed off of my lap, I looked up at the screen and watched as the new Admiral Plural shook hands with the senior officers. The love of Jenna Plural radiated in my heart. "We finally have a chance of winning this war, Helen, and she's going to lead us to it."

I did not look back as I heard Helen sigh again, "I hope so, Emma, I really do."

CHAPTER FIFTEEN

DESTINATION ENCELADUS

My Commission came through the following day. I was now Emma Dodgson, Lieutenant First Class. I was surprised that I had not only received a commission but skipped a rank. I was now the same rank as Jenna Plural when I first met her.

I was made to attend officer training classes supervised under the office of Commodore Addison. Mr. Phelkar was sorry to see me go from his staff, but even his work had been winding down as more and more of his duties got turned over to Addison. The classes were rather dull and more about protocol than leadership, although they tried to convince me the two were intertwined. I was assigned offices and the batman of my own. Luke Pennington. He was about my age and until now, had served as a naval steward. However, he fell into the world of bureaucracy quite easily and always had the coffee ready when I arrived in the morning. Addison told me that I had the pick of any personnel with few exceptions. Such as, I couldn't pick Helen Tracker as my tech as she was now the head of fleet technology. The major positions to fill were the unit were Sergeant, vehicle specialist, tech specialist, and weapons specialist. Finding the tech specialist was the easy part. I simply asked Helen to pick someone from her team and assign her to me. I did get one shock. When I requested an exceptionally able demolition expert, I found I was stonewalled. Katherine Andreas was an army veteran of about seven years. She was legendary among ordnance personnel for her ability to control explosives like it was an art form. However, when I filed the paperwork and sent it to her current commanding officer, I received a very curt response. Andreas was an essential part of his team, and he couldn't possibly spare her and thanked me for my interest.

I wasn't too sure how to react to this. As an enlisted grunt, I was used to being told no, but I've never been in a position before where I was told I could do something, and then someone else would refuse. So I took the issue to Addison, but she was far from sympathetic.

"Of course, he doesn't want to give up his best personnel," She told me curtly, "No one would; however, you have been given the authority to recruit her to your team, and you need to use that authority. You cannot come to me whenever you face a hurdle. Now go get your demolitions officer."

Easier said than done. I was not ready for a confrontation with a senior officer, no matter how much authority I had been given. It had been bludgeoned into me from the day I joined the marines that I take orders not to give them, and it was hard getting past that.

So, steeling myself, I sent him a reply stating that the transfer of Katherine Andreas was not a request and that I expected it to happen in the next few days. I then moved on to recruiting my other personnel, which was not so problematic.

A couple of days later, Andreas's commanding officer had not replied. It was my move again. So I looked up to see where he was stationed. It was the USS Minneapolis, and I arranged a fleet shuttle to transport me there. However, upon arrival, he refused to see me stating he was too busy. This information was relayed to me through his assistant. To be honest, I felt somewhat flummoxed. It was quite a quandary. The man outranked me. Yes, my authority came directly from Addison, but...

I decided to bluff. Looking the PA straight in the eye, I said, "very well, although I'm sure Admiral Plural will be most disappointed in his failure to assist me."

I then headed out to the shuttle dock but was barely down the corridor when the PA caught up with me. "It would appear that the captain has found a space in his itinerary and can see you now."

I grinned, then composed myself with a grim face before I turned back to him. I followed him back into the reception, and he led me to a back office.

The first words out of the mouth of the elderly Captain Tanner were, "you can't have her. She's a vital part of my team and does not want to leave anyway."

I raised an eyebrow, and after a dramatic pause, I replied, "on the latter part of that, isn't it irrelevant? While the choices of personnel can be considered, they're not the deciding factor in any posting. On the former, I have been given liberty to choose any personnel for my team that I wish."

He glared at me, his face reddening with anger. "You are barely out of diapers, Lieutenant. I have run this unit for twenty years, and we are an elite tactical team."

I raised a questioning eyebrow, "I may be barely out of diapers, Captain, but I *am* out of them."

"I will not have my team broken up by some little upstart bitch, especially a damn genmod."

My eyes narrowed. "I would choose your words more carefully, captain. You sound like an insurrectionist, and that's not something tolerated."

"When you manage to dry your ears, Lieutenant, you learn that obedience to the chain of command does not mean you have to agree with that chain of command."

"You are right. However, you are obligated to maintain respect, captain. Jenna Plural is our leader, whether you like it or not, and I am commissioned to put together a team of which Katherine Andreas will be part. If you wish me to take this higher, I will, but trust me, neither Admiral Plural nor Commodore Addison will appreciate being dragged into what should be a simple crew redistribution issue. Am I making myself clear, Sir?"

He glared at me and looked as though he was going to protest further but gave up. "I will complete the paperwork tomorrow and send Katherine to you."

"I would appreciate it if you would do it today, as time is of the essence." It wasn't. We had no mission prep, and several of my team had to complete duties before moving over to the Constitution, but I wanted to push this little poop head.

"Very well, Lieutenant." He sat back in his chair and heaved a weary sigh, "I'm getting too old for all this bull shit. I should have retired several years ago."

"That might have been a good idea, Sir, as it is no longer an option."

"What is that supposed to mean?" He narrowed his eyes at me.

"Well, Sir, the fleet is no longer getting supplied from Earth, and resources will be stretched thin. There'll be no room for passengers, is all I'm saying." Before he could respond, I concluded the conversation. "I expect to see Andreas before the end of the week. If I don't, I will list her as AWOL and order her immediate arrest. Do we have an understanding?"

I waited for the reply, but he simply said, "you are dismissed, Lieutenant."

I smiled, thanked him, and returned to the USS Constitution.

My Sergeant came as the result of a recommendation by Captain Addison. Audra Pentauk had recently been serving under the recently promoted Stacey Grant, but this was hardly a reference for me. However, I considered it inappropriate not to accept my commanding officer's suggestion. I picked off the rest of my team, and I received no further direct objections but did hear that complaints were being sent up the line to Addison, who, I understand, did not respond to them in a very friendly manner.

With everything complete, I sent my list up to Addison for the formality of her stamp of approval. It was done and dusted. I was commander of a new elite force of commandos. Now I had to turn them into a team.

Winning over the hearts and minds of your troops is probably the hardest task for an officer in any military branch. It is not enough that you get their obedience. You have to get their trust, which does not mean becoming their friend. However, an officer's most powerful tool is their Sergeant. If the Sergeant can work well with you and your people, you're halfway there. Pentauk turned out to be an excellent Sergeant with the right mix of authority and approach for this.

When I first met the team, they looked like a little ragtag bunch. I had taken them from all Navy, Army, Air force, and Marine Corps services. I had scheduled a meeting in one of the many cargo holds on the Constitution to begin our first prep sessions. I still did not have an officer's uniform, so I arrived in combat fatigues with my corporal stripes removed.

Another hill I had to climb was that I was an officer via a field commission. Many troops have a hard time seeing formally enlisted personnel as commanding officers.

As I entered, they were all sitting around the room chatting away. The team was fourteen in total, and I'm not going to name them all unless it becomes important as I progress. For the most part, just try to remember Pentauk and Andreas. The moment she saw me, Pentauk barked out for everyone to stand to attention. They did so in a strict military fashion except for one. A short girl in her late twenties with a shaggy mane of badly waived hair and thick eyeliner sluggishly got to her feet. I chose to ignore it for now and introduced myself. "Ladies and gentlemen, I am Lieutenant Dodgson, your new commanding officer, as I'm sure you're already aware. This unit has been commissioned at the direct request of Admiral Plural. It is my intent not to let her down. We will become the ultimate fighting unit in this flotilla. We will be the first on the ground and the last to leave. We will go where no one else would dare go. You are the best, but you're gonna be better."

The short girl raised her hand. I don't know if she thought she was in high school, but I decided to indulge her. "Yes, what is it?"

"Meaning no disrespect, ma'am," she said, meaning she was just about to disrespect me. "While I readily admit we are the best. I'm wondering how someone who's not a year out of boot camp will command us. Especially one who cannot even give a coherent order." She was, of course, referring to my speech impediment, which, as I have already told you, I am ignoring in telling this tale. It was commented on constantly. However, on this occasion, I will address it as it was a concern of mine. My stammer got worse when I was stressed, and nothing was more stressful than a combat situation, and I was afraid it would fail me in the field.

Pentauk was about to put her down, but I raised her hand. "What is your name, corporal?"

"Andreas." She replied.

177

Ah, of course, it was. "A fair question. We're in a transitional period. Many people need to get used to the new chain of command and our new leader. Some even think we should capitulate to the enemy. I have proven myself to the Admiral, and she has chosen me more out of my loyalty than my experience. I do not need to know how to do the things you know. I just need to know what needs to be done. I do not ask you to trust me, but I ask you to give me the chance to earn your trust. As for my stammer, it will not be an issue."

"That sounds good," Andreas said but added, "if you are arranging a picnic, but we're putting our lives on the line here, we can't worry about trusting you on the battlefield." A few murmurings of agreement flittered around the room.

"I understand your concern. However, these are desperate times, and we cannot expect things to go along the way they used to. We have to adapt to survive. We have no home base. No one is going to refill our ammunition. No supplies are coming from Earth or any of the other colonies. At least not yet. We are in the greatest fight of our lives. We do, or we die. However, put your faith in me, and I will not prove faithless."

The girl nodded, "If you are so confident, would you be willing to do a deal with us?"

"I'm willing to listen to what you want to propose?" I said uneasily.

"If we do one mission with you and after that, we're uncomfortable with your command. You allow us to decide whether to stay with you or not." She locked eyes with me.

I pondered this. "It is rather orthodox, and my superiors will not like it, but yes, I am confident enough to do that deal with you."

Addison did not like it. She chewed me out for fifteen minutes before she even let me speak. "I do not know what Jenna will say about this."

"To be honest, ma'am, I didn't plan on telling her." I smiled, but Addison did not reciprocate. "They raised some good points about my experience, and to be honest, I think I need to prove myself to them, to you, and the Admiral."

Addison sighed, "Maybe you're right. I don't think so, but I'm going to trust you on this."

"Think of it this way, Commodore. If our mission succeeds, they will want to stay with me. If it fails, we will be all dead."

Addison grinned. "Fair point."

A couple of days later, I was summoned to a conference meeting with Admiral Plural. Present with her was Addison, Kensett, and Helen. A technician called Ryan Baxter was also present at the request of Helen.

I felt somewhat excited because it was clear that this would be a mission briefing. My first true test of command.

"As you know, one of our biggest problems is that we don't have a base," Admiral Plural began. "While we have some ships that can be converted into farming galleries, it won't be sufficient to support us. In addition, the manufacturing of ammunition and weaponry is also a consideration. Even if we were victorious in every battle, losing one or two ships every time will ultimately whittle us down to nothing." She activated the large screen on the wall. It was filled with the picture of an icy world. "This is Enceladus. A moon of Saturn lying within its rings. It is also an American base with diverse manufacturing operations designed to supply the outer world colonies. However, since the surrender, it has gone radio silent. It does not respond to our calls. We do not know if European forces have occupied it or simply that the Americans have hunkered down to wait this out or even if they are now actively accepting European commands as part of the surrender. It is a highly secure facility with about six thousand people. So it's more than just a production site or military installation. It is a living, breathing community." She looked back at me. "Your mission, Lieutenant Dodgson, is to take your team in there and find out what's happening. However, I am leaving the mission open-ended, and how we proceed will be based on your report. You may find they remain loyal. There may be a European presence, or they may simply remain independent. Either way, I intend to take Enceladus and make it part of the new Confederation. We need that base and its production facilities and the ability to land the ships capable of landing to maintain fueling station, etcetera."

She returned to her seat as Addison got up to continue the briefing. "The base is heavily armed. It has anti-aircraft weaponry, so we cannot drop you actually at the base and will be compelled to drop you several miles away. This area of space is also heavily patrolled by European forces, mostly French and some German. As a result, we will be using the captured Peon shuttle piloted by Captain Grant, accompanied by Mr. Phelkar, for his fluency in French. They will drop you off without landing, only returning if the mission is aborted. Of course, we hope to land and meet you there if successful. You'll have to track across the icy wastes facing obstacles such as chasms and freezing temperatures below anything you could possibly encounter on Earth. It's not going to be an easy trip."

She returned to her seat, and Helen got up. "When you reach the base getting in is not going to be easy either. The base is not designed for people to walk in and out. Most exits are for people to maintain repairs outside and conduct surveys and other experiments. It is pretty sealed off. Most doors should be heavily guarded. What is not heavily guarded but still sealed off are the exhaust tubes. They pump out any noxious gases or chemicals produced in the base, and we believe we can get you in there through the access tunnels used for maintenance. Of course, the doors will be locked, so I asked Ryan to be here. He is one of my best techs, or rather he is now one of *your* best techs." Ryan smiled at me, and I smiled back. "It will be his job to bypass the security of the doors and get you in. I'll provide him with equipment to assist with this task." She sat back down, and Jenna rose once more.

"As I said, I do not know what you will find there. If possible, contact the American leadership and find out where their loyalties lie. If possible, have them contact me, and I will have Mr. Phelkar begin negotiations with them for some sort of agreement, or they may even outright join us. If not, you are to appraise the situation and gain as much information for us to take the base by force with a minimal amount of damage and loss of life. I'm going to give you a free hand here, Dodgson, to do what you think is necessary to find the easiest way to take Enceladus. If we don't hear from you within four days, it will be assumed you are dead, and we will reassess the situation. However, while you are there, there is a secondary objective."

She yielded the floor for Charlotte Kensett. "The base has another purpose. It is an outpost of the United States Department of Defense Research Division. Albeit through a private sector contact with Grant Industries." An image of an elderly man came up on the screen. "This is Doctor Benton McKay, a senior researcher in M.E.T. technology. Prior to the capitulation, my sources informed me that he had made some major breakthroughs. I don't know what, but we believe they could be very useful for the war effort. If possible, you ought to locate and extract this man."

"What if he does not cooperate?" I asked.

"You extract him with or without his cooperation," said the Admiral casually. "However, this is a secondary objective, and I will leave it to you to decide if it can be done without jeopardizing the primary mission ." She looked around the table. "I believe we have covered everything." There were general nods of agreement. "Very well. Do you require any clarification on anything, Lieutenant Dodgson?" I advised her that there was not. "In that case, this meeting is closed. Dodgson, stay awhile." As the room cleared, I found myself sitting alone opposite the greatest woman who ever lived. She waited patiently until the door closed and then looked at me. "How are you holding up, Dodgson?"

"I'm doing very well, ma'am."

"I have to tell you I have received a lot of flak from my advisors for giving you a commission and placing you in such a position of authority. I stand by my decision. I made it clear that I have complete and utter faith in you. This mission will not just reflect on you but also on me. Fuck this up, and I will look like an idiot." Her steely gaze locked on me. "And Dodgson, I *really* don't want to look like an idiot. Are we clear?"

"I will not let you down, ma'am. You have my word on that." I said with all genuine sincerity.

Her affectionate smile returned. "I'm confident that you won't. I just wanted to reiterate how important this mission is. Good luck, Dodgson. You are dismissed."

Rumors that Stacey Grant had got Phelkar into trouble in the ship's ventilation shaft started to travel around. It made the captain even less endearing than I found her before. Men are weak individuals when it comes to seduction. Even someone as honorable as Mr. Phelkar could fall afoul of the serpent in the garden of Eden. Using her feminine wiles to seduce such a man and bring him down to her level disgusted me. However, it was made worse by the fact that she was doing it to the man our leader had claimed his her own. Surely, for as long as Jenna Plural was interested in him, he should have been off-limits to everyone. She was worse than Jezebel. She was Eve tempting him with her apples.

With great reluctance, I was compelled to work with her on this mission. Fortunately, I did not have to engage in conversation with her, and we piled into the back of the shuttle. She and Mr. Phelkar sat in the cockpit. My team strapped themselves into their seats.

I sat there looking through the door at Mr. Phelkar and the Jezebel. We were supposed to slip out amongst the traffic with our trip being an unregistered and unreported departure to ensure prying eyes did not know what we were doing. As we waited, I saw her looking at him, and I felt a pang of anger. Grant needed to be eliminated for the good of all, and I pondered when I would get my chance.

We waited over an hour until Grant found the opportunity to slip in behind another craft. We drifted out of the dock on dark energy repulsors. She then set a course for Enceladus, and we were on our way.

Chapter Sixteen

The Icy Wastes of Heck

As Stacey Grant brought us down over the drop zone, she called back, telling us to get ready. She would have to drop us several miles from our target to avoid detection. We geared ourselves up in tactical EMU suits checking each other seals. Then Grant sealed the cockpit door, and we all stood waiting for her call. When it came, I nodded to Pentauk, who nodded back and opened the outer door. As the vacuum enveloped us, everything went silent. My team's breathing over the comm lines was the only thing that could be heard. Standing by the opening, I looked down at the sheer white mass of ground before us. Our first order of business was to push out the equipment we needed. I then pulled the lever that released the bottom of the secondary cargo bay beneath us and dropped the all-terrain vehicle we hoped would get as close as possible to the American community.

I slapped my first team member on the back, and he jumped out. Each followed in quick succession until finally, Pentauk went to. I was alone and looked back at the door where Phelkar and Jezebel now hid behind. I sighed softly and then followed my team out of the doorway.

The gravity of Enceladus was so low that there was no need for any form of decent apparatus. A parachute wouldn't work because there was no air, but there was neither the need for DE compensators. The descent was slow enough that we could land on our feet without assistance and completely unharmed. As I went down, I watched for all the different places I could see my team coming down. The ground was coming closer at a very slow rate. To give Grant her due, she had found the perfect place for our landing, a flat icy plane that stretched onto the horizon. Eventually, I landed on my toes and turned around to take in my surroundings. Although we were on a flat plain, the planetary body was so small that the horizon disappeared quickly. I could only see two or three of my people. I activated my comlink. "Dodgson down and safe. By the numbers, all check-in." Slowly but surely, each person checked in with me. Although the likelihood of casualties or injury at this stage was unlikely, I felt relief as everyone confirmed a safe landing. "Pentauk, bring everyone into the terrain vehicle."

"Yes, ma'am," came her reply, and she quickly snapped orders to the other troops and transmitted the vehicle's locator beacon. I looked up into the sky. I could make out the dim light of Grant's shuttle as it disappeared back up into space. I then checked the vehicle's location myself and headed in that direction. The walk to the vehicle took about twenty minutes across the sheet of ice, and it was lucky the spikes in my boots could grip its surface; otherwise, it would have been like trying to cross over an ice rink. I met up with two of my men en route, and slowly but surely, we all came together at the large vehicle. It had landed on its side, but it did not take any effort to push it over onto its treads. All but two of us climbed inside, and Pentauk took the driver seat as I slipped into a chair amongst my men lined up against the wall. Pentauk turned on the engine and checked the navigation system, and slowly we started to move out.

The first order of business was to pick up our equipment, and we spent about an hour following the locator signals with the two troops jumping off of the vehicle to grab the equipment and stack it on the roof.

"That's the last of them," Pentauk informed me.

The two men on the roof climbed inside. When the entry hatch was sealed, Pentauk released air into the vehicle, and once the computer beeped confirmation that it was safe to do so, we all started to remove our helmets

"Let's head out toward the base, Sargent," I commanded.

"Yes, ma'am." she replied and a few moments later added, "Course laid in. We are on our way."

The vehicle was not very fast. It was designed to get over difficult terrain, not to rush us into battle. My troops engaged in idle chatter as we traveled, but I did not engage. I was startled when I heard a constant pounding of some things hitting our roof very lightly. I rose from my seat and went to the front, slipping into the passenger seat beside Pentauk. "What the heck is that.?"

"I think it's ice, Ma'am. Look." She pointed ahead and to the left. Looking out, I could see the massive geysers erupting. What was hitting us was ice slowly falling upon us. "The beauty of God's creation is beyond description."

I was unaware that I had said this out loud until Pentauk replied, "you can say that again, ma'am. Wow!"

Indeed I cannot describe the beauty of this moment. I don't have the fancy words of Mr. Phelkar or even the colorful descriptiveness of Stacey Grant. You just have to trust me. This was amazing to behold. Disappearing into space, these geysers belched forth water from the planet's core. I continued to stare at it as we moved along, and my team took turns coming up and looking from the doorway of the vehicle cockpit. Their gasps of awe pretty much summed up everything. Then the land began to become hilly and then rocky. The vehicle began to struggle, and I decided it was time we should stop for the night.

Slipping back to my team and retaking my seat with them, Pentauk joined us. I had one of the privates break out the rations and serve them to everyone. Solid blocks of neutrophil gunk. Tasteless and barely digestible. "Well, it's not the most comfortable place to sleep, but do your best it's probably the last chance we're going to get until this mission is over," I told them. They were all veterans and would not exactly be unused to sleeping in strange unusual places.

I didn't get much sleep, not because of discomfort but because my mind was on the mission ahead and not know-ing what we would find. Part of me was eager to find the base intact with the welcoming arms of American civilians, but another part was eager to put my training to use and fight our way to the heart of the community.

As dawn approached, I made my way up to the passenger seat at the front of the vehicle. I say dawn, but I refer to the time on our watches rather than the positioning of the moon we were on. I gasped as I could now see Saturn overhead. The most beautiful sight in the solar system filled the sky. Pentauk soon joined me, and she was also taken in by the sight, with a broad smile on her face. I smiled at her. "Let's get moving, corporal."

"Yes, ma'am."

Had this been on Earth, there was no way that the vehicle would have made it up over the mountainous terrain we now traversed, but with the low gravity, Pentauk was able to bounce it over the more tricky or steep areas. When we finally reached the top, we stopped and looked down across the wastes to see the vast dome structure of the American base. It was hard to get a perspective of how far away it was with the curvature of a moon this size and the lack of any other topography. I had to look down at the navigation screen to be told how many miles away it was. However, what caused me to sigh was the site of a chasm between us and the base. It was not particularly big, but big enough that there was no way the terrain vehicle could jump it even if I wanted to try, which I didn't.

Pentauk moaned. "It was too good to be true for this to remain a smooth ride, ma'am." She muttered.

"Agreed." I chuckled. "Come on, get us down there as close as you can, and I will let the team know what's happening once we are there."

"Yes, ma'am."

The mountainous outcropping's descent down the other side proved harder than the actual climb. It was only the consummate skill of Audra Pentauk that stopped us from bouncing off of it. Slowly but surely, we reached the glacial plane again. It took about another hour to reach the chasm, but I did not need to inform the team, for all the bouncing around had ensured everyone was awake.

Pentauk scanned the topography to ensure that the closer we got to the edge of the chasm, the ice remained solid for us. She ultimately got us just a few feet away from the edge.

"Okay, this is as far as we go with the vehicle. We're going to have to abandon it here. Hopefully, we can pick it up again once our mission is over." By the look on the faces of my team, they didn't give a poop about leaving the vehicle behind. I was thinking about the fleet's limited resources and that abandoning such useful equipment on a single mission was a waste.

We resealed our helmets, and once more, the hatch was opened. Pentauk went first, followed by my team, and finally myself. It looked weird and silly to see my team putting equipment packs on their backs that were four or five times the size and weight of what they could carry on Earth. I jumped off the roof with no more difficulty than if I was stepping off a sidewalk curb. I walked up to the edge of the chasm and looked down, my stomach queasy at seeing the long drop into darkness. Then looking across to the other side, about twenty feet away. I turned and waved one of my people forward to join me. "Do you think you could get a harpoon into that side?" I asked.

He looked at me quizically. "Sure, ma'am, but with this gravity, we could just jump it."

I hope he couldn't see me blush at my stupidity when he said this. I would surely not forget him humiliating me this way. "Show me," I said coldly and stretched out my hand to indicate across the chasm.

He nodded, taking a run; he jumped into the air sailing up a considerable distance before he started her descent, clearing the chasm by at least a further twenty feet. With that, I waved off the rest of my team, and one by one, they leapt over to the other side, with me bringing up the rear. As I floated across, it felt strange as I arced and went down again, landing nimbly upon my toes. Then we made the steady march toward the base. As we got close, I tried to communicate with it again by radio, but all I got back was static. Slowly the dome grew in size, and eventually, we stood at its outer wall.

I studied it for a short time before turning to Katherine Andreas and saying, "how about the possibility of blowing a hole in this wall for us to get inside?"

She looked at me incredulously. "Even if I could, which I can't, you would cause decompression and kill anyone on the other side," she said, causing others in the group to chuckle, much to my further humiliation. "However, these domes are designed to resist an aerial bombardment, so I wouldn't even scratch it with the ordinance I have."

"It was just an idea," I muttered.

"Yes, ma'am," she replied in a most condescending tone. I caught the gaze of Pentauk, who was looking at me and wide-eyed disbelief.

I started walking along the outside of the wall. I got quite a distance before looking back and seeing my team was still standing where I'd left them. "Come on," I commanded. They looked at each other before very begrudgingly following on. We continued for about an hour until we came to one of the exhaust ports we had been told about. Its vast jet was chugging away silently, and a faint green plume was expelled. This would be a fan on Earth, but with no air, such a device was useless here. Instead, everything was suctioned out.

"I was hoping this wasn't going to be active," I said to Pentauk on a private line.

"Well, at least it means this base is operational. There *are* people inside." She replied. With no air being expelled, walking up to the fan in a vacuum proved very easy, and I spotted the small maintenance hatch leading through to an airlock at its side.

I turned to Andreas. "Is there a problem with blowing this?" I said sarcastically.

"You could try just opening it first. That's why we bought a tech, isn't it?" she said irritably.

It was my turn to be vitriolic as I replied, "there is no way to open it on this side." It did not get the laugh I intended, which irritated me, but I took my victory anyway.

"Okay, everybody. Stand back," Andreas said. "You won't see or hear it, but y'all damn well feel it if you get in its way."

We all backed out, went around the corner, and waited impatiently while she set up her explosives. Minutes later, she came and joined us and stood with arms folded, glaring at me for a reason I could not comprehend. Sixty seconds later, pieces of debris flew out silently into our view.

I slipped my officer's pistol from my holster and nodded for the others to ready their rifles. "Okay, team, we have access to Enceladus Base. We will enter with caution. And be ready for anything. For flip sake, don't shoot any civilians regardless of nationality."

"How in hell are we gonna know the nationality of civilians?" Andreas said to the laughter of the rest of the team. I was *really* starting to hate this girl.

I just replied, "move out."

We headed back into the vent, stepped over the debris caused by his explosions, and entered Enceladus Base.

Chapter Seventeen

Techs

The darkened corridor ended at the opening of the airlock. I stood aside as the technician Baxter, stepped up to the door. It took only a couple of minutes, the tech stepped back, and the door swung open. And we all entered the airlock. The door closed behind us, and the compartment started repressurizing and filling with air automatically. I reached out to unfasten my helmet, but Pentauk suddenly grabbed my arm. "Ma'am, we have no idea what the conditions are on the other side of that door we could depress again." My team began muttering and chattering until Pentauk snapped, "shut it, troopers." Silence fell once more, and I realized I was losing any hope of respect from this group and would need to do something soon to restore my authority. The technician worked on the inner airlock, and there was that slight hiss as the door came open and the different air met each other. This led us to a maintenance shaft.

The shaft was large enough for us to walk upright. And we continued along it for about ten minutes. We found the door at the end, but it was sealed from the other side. I hesitated, ensuring I had checked all our options before turning back to Andreas. I nodded, and we all stepped back out of her way as she came forward. She stared at the door for a moment, then looked back at me and shook her head. "This door is at least six inches thick. It's designed to withstand decompression explosives. If I blow this, that won't leave much of this shaft behind, and we'll kill ourselves."

I sighed and bit my lip, pondering what to do next. Some will say it was a coincidence, but I know better. It was divine intervention that the door began to open, and there stood a surprised-looking tech in overalls and an ungainly tool kit about her belt. She could not have been older than me, and she slowly raised her hands with wide eyes at the sight of our weapons trained on her. "Oh dear!" she muttered softly.

"Name, rank, and number." Pentauk barked at her.

"Amy Bessinger." She replied in a voice that could only be described as fear as Pentauk slowly and gently guided her back so we could step through the entrance. "I'm a civilian and don't have a rank or number." She hesitated. "Well, unless you want my social? But I am a first technician if that helps?"

I looked down at her belt to check for a weapon, but it was simply full of various tools for her work. However, I did not relax. "We are with The United States Mar...." I started to say until Pentauk corrected me with a cough. "I mean the Solar Confederation Special Operations Team. We are here to claim this base."

Amy looked at me with wide eyes and gave me a little shrug. "Well, Okay then," she said softly.

Again I realized how stupid I was announcing this to what was little more than a grease monkey. "Are you able to take me to someone in a position of authority?"

"Well, I can take you to my manager," she replied. "Though I'm not sure he can help you any more than I can."

"Please don't hurt her." I spun about with my weapon to see a young man approaching, his hands raised in a peace gesture. Tall, Hispanic with gentle features, and dressed similarly to Bessinger.

"Identify yourself," I demanded

"Angel Mendez. Senior technician," he said abruptly. "I should warn you. You will not get a warm welcome here. The hierarchy of this base has taken advantage of the surrender to become fully independent."

"But this is a research and industrial base. It's not even a colony." Pentauk said, stepping up beside me.

"Well, it's a little more than that," Mendez said uneasily.

"Explain," I said curtly

"May I ask that you lower those weapons? I can't speak for Amy here, but I consider myself a loyal American. I want to help if I can, but I am not sure what I can do."

"Hey, if you can get me out of here, you can count me in, too," Amy said eagerly.

"Well, there are two different definitions of a loyal American these days," I said cautiously.

"I'm not sure what you mean." Mendez frowned.

"Do you support or oppose the surrender of the United States and the Pacific alliance?" I asked.

"Ah, now that is a question where you'll shoot me if I don't answer correctly?" He said uneasily.

"Possibly. But I would almost definitely shoot you if you don't answer." I smiled at him when I said this.

"Well, it's rather a game of Russian roulette then, isn't it? Here is my answer. I support whoever has the best interests of my people at heart. I am yet to be convinced either side has our best interests at the forefront of their minds."

"Fair enough." I gestured for my team to lower their weapons, and they complied. Mendez sighed with relief, and he and Bessenger then led us back to a small warehouse filled with broken equipment, which the techs were working on repairing. Several others stopped working and stood up to stare at us as we entered. Soon a small group was gathered around us.

"After the fall, the powers that be closed us off from all contact." Mendez was telling us. "Things here are not what you would expect."

"Shut up, Mendez. You're going to get us all killed." An older woman snapped at him.

"Do you want to stay on this rock for the rest of your life, Kendra?" Amy snapped back. Kendra hesitated and was about to say something but backed down and lowered her head.

Mendez looked back at me, "For several years, this base has been used by an illegal cartel. The primary research here is weaponry, and a black market has been running out of here unchallenged for the longest time."

"How is that even possible?" Pentauk said. "To even land here, you had to have high-security clearance."

"Yes," Amy laughed. "And in an ideal solar system, there'll be no such thing as government corruption. We are not living in an ideal solar system. Anyway, we are not really government. The base is, or rather was, operated by a corporate contract."

"What company?" I asked.

"Grant Industries. Until the US surrender, we received all instructions from the corporate office of Hannah Grant."

"Grant Industries is involved in the illegal activities here?" Pentauk asked.

"No idea." Amy shrugged. "Grant Industries transports have been used, but whether the company knows it is anyone's guess."

"What is the nature of the legal activity here," I asked as I sat at an empty table and indicated to my team to relax.

"On the minor side, we are talking about smuggling goods for tax evasion," Kenra spoke. "Ships stop here and unload their cargo. Another ship picks them up and takes them to the next port of call."

"And on the major side?" Pentauk asked.

"Tech running."

My eyes widened. Tech running was a serious crime. It was selling military tech to the private sector or even possibly the enemy. Anything from small arms to computer systems and missile weaponry. At best, it was theft and unlicenced arms dealing; at its worst, it became treason.

"Okay, what are we talking about here?"

"Schematics," Mendez said quietly as if we could be overheard. I shrugged and looked questioningly at him, not knowing what he was talking about other than the definition of the word schematics. "Research is conducted here on developing new and interesting ways to kill each other, and then the plans get sold in a black market auction to the highest bidder."

"How could the US government not notice it is not getting the tech that it's paid for?" Pentauk asked.

"Oh, it gets it eventually, maybe a year or two after the schematics have been sold. It's not exactly hard to delay research or at least show that research has been delayed."

"Are you telling me that there's tech here that could have helped us win this war being held back for someone's bank balance?" I asked, unable to hide my irritation.

"Well, that's how it worked over the last few years, so yes, I guess there is probably tech here that has been held back. Obviously, someone of my level does not know the specifics." Mendez told me.

I glanced at Pentauk, who looked seriously shocked, but I remembered something and looked back at Bessinger and Mendez. "My secondary mission is to find a scientist called McKay. He's supposedly researching advanced M. E.T. technology. Do you know him?"

He glanced uneasily at Bessinger, who looked down at her feet guiltily. "Not much more than a good morning basis, but yes, I know him," he replied.

"I need to see him."

"Well, good luck with that. But as soon as the powers that be find out you're here, they will be out to kill you," Amy said. "They see the war's end as a profit loss and believe that by going independent, they can take advantage of the emerging nations out of the chaos."

"Exactly who are these powers that be," Pentauk asked.

"The science quorum," Amy answered.

"Well, I hardly think a bunch of scientists will have much effect against us," I said, more hopeful than convinced.

"Yeah, I don't think you understand," Mendez said, almost sounding conspiratorial. "They were not really in control. It's a cartel front, and with the considerable stipend paid out under the counter to the security staff, they have their unwavering loyalty."

"Even so," Pentauk stated. "We must take out this quorum and gain control of this base. Can I assume you would be willing to help us in that endeavor?"

He hesitated and glanced at Amy. She nodded back at him and said, "if it's going to get us off this rock, then I'm in." she said determinedly, and there were a few murmurs of approval around her.

Mendes sighed. "Well, it would appear that Enceladus Space Tech Division Two is at your service, ma'am."

About an hour later, we had got out of our EMU suits, and the techs had fed us. It was nice to have something that wasn't basic military fare. We were relaxed and drinking coffee as we carried on talking.

"What is the military complement of this base?" Pentauk asked.

"Actually, none," Mendez informed us. "When the surrender of the United States came over the line, our army contingent bugged out."

"Why didn't you go with them," I asked.

Mendez looked at me as if that was a strange question, but he replied casually. "Enceladus Base may not be much, and it may not be the most hospitable place in the solar system, but it is our home. Most of us have been here ten years or more, and we've raised our families here. Why would we want to go somewhere else?"

I could think of a hundred different reasons, but I replied, "I understand. However, I take it that you did not expect your current circumstances to happen?"

"No, our main concern was this base being taken by the Peons. With the military gone, there was no one to man the defenses." And that, I realized, was why no one fired upon us coming in, but I said nothing and let Mendez continue. "There was a lot of talk about declaring independence, but then the science quorum and the cartel had that big falling out. Most of the science divisions have barricaded themselves in the outer ring of the base."

"Why didn't you go with them since they are not the criminal element?" Pentauk asked

Mendez snorted with derision, "because the cartel basically told us we couldn't and made the consequences of us trying to very clear."

"We should tell them, Angel," Amy said. He sighed and nodded. "We have been running an underground railroad to get scientists out of cartel hands to where they are blocked off in the outer ring," advised Amy. "As it happens, there is one called name McKay. The one you asked about."

I sat up, interested. "Where can I find him?"

Amy was about to answer, but Mendez suspiciously said, "why do you want him? "

I had no obligation to answer this question, but I doubted he would continue helping us if I didn't. "He's working on some tech my superior is interested in obtaining."

Mendez sighed. "So that's the real reason you are here?"

"No, Sir," Pentauk put in quickly. "It is an objective of ours, but it is a secondary objective."

"Be honest with me, and I will be more helpful," Mendez responded. "What is your true objective?"

Pentauk looked at me. I sighed and answered him. "We intend to make Enceledas a base part of the Solar Confederation. A place where we can repair our ships, rotate personnel, and call a center of operations for the new war effort. The fight back to Earth has begun."

"And what about us?" Amy asked uneasily.

I fixed my eyes upon her determinedly to ensure she took me seriously. "Your skills will be invaluable to us. There is a place for you in the Confederation, and we will value that."

Mendez shook his head. "We are tired of war. It is over, and we just want to live in peace."

"Do you think the Peons will let you live in peace?" Pentauk asked intently.

"They would take over this base with their military and use the research done here against us," I said. "Your fellow

Americans. There will be no peace. It would just be about which side you are on."

Mendez did not respond to this, only looking at Amy with a dejected sigh as Pentauk added, "the biggest difference will be that you are volunteers if you work with us. The Peons won't give you that option."

"I guess it is too much to ask that you would just leave us in peace?" Mendez said bitterly.

I balked at this. "You want us to liberate you from your cartel using *our* lives and *our* resources and expect us just to leave?"

"Even if we did do that," Pentauk said. "How long do you think it will be before the European Union starts landing ships here and taking over? You have two choices. Become puppets for the Peons or join the force fighting for your liberty in the hope that one day you will be free to live here in peace."

Amy gave Mendez a sideways look. "They have a point, Angel. We heard that speech broadcast by Jenna Plural. She is standing up for us in a way the US government never has."

Mendez sighed again and raised his hands in resignation. "Fine. What would you have us do, Lieutenant?"

"We need to take out this Quorum's hierarchy. It should not be difficult if they do not have military support." I replied.

"They still have some civilian security forces. They are pretty much mercenaries, and we call them Rent-A-Cops."

"What sort of armaments do they have?" Pentauk asked.

"Standard police issue weaponry, I would think," Mendez replied.

Pentauk looked at me. "Handguns, assault rifles, shotguns," she said as if reading off a shopping list.

"Agreed. However, they do not have our training. Still, we should proceed with the greatest caution." I looked back at Mendez and Amy. "Is there any way we can get to the administration center without encountering opposition?"

Mendez shook his head. "Most of the travel around this base is in pods through the transit tubes, but they're pretty locked down by the cartel."

"Can you get them running for us?"

He pondered this as he looked at Amy before looking back at me. "There is only one person here with that expertise, and I'm not letting you take her."

Amy looked quite annoyed and turned on him aggressively. "You may be senior tech here, but I think you can't speak for me in these circumstances."

"I don't want you getting killed, Amy," Mendez told her, looking a little embarrassed by her reaction.

"Look, let's be honest," Amy responded. "I know you have had the hots for me for a long time, but you should have gotten the message by now that it's never going to happen. This is not a decision based on your personal interest in me."

Mendez colored slightly and responded with a stammer that made mine look quite mild. I could not understand him, but Amy was not about to let him speak. She turned back to me. "Lieutenant," her voice was firm and determined. "I can bypass the lockouts. But I can't get it not to register on the central administration's computer systems. If we do this, they will know we are coming and that you got help from us."

"Do you know any alternative?" I asked.

"We can always go through the maintenance shafts, but that would take you hours, and it's highly unlikely we will get through undetected since various cameras monitor what goes on in there at various points."

I looked to Pentauk for her opinion. She looked back at Amy. "How long would it take a pod to get to the central administration?" She asked Amy.

"About fifteen minutes," Amy replied.

Pentauk looked back at me. "They will know we are coming, but they won't have much time to mount a defense, and they won't necessarily know it's a military unit. Just that someone has activated one of these pods."

"However dangerous it sounds, it still seems like the safest option." I looked back to Mendez. "I really would like to see McKay, if it is at all possible."

He nodded and rose to his feet. "Come with me." He led Pentauk and me over to a large cargo container and opened the door. I looked at Pentauk, confused, and she just shrugged back at me. As we followed him into the dark, he lit a flashlight, and we could see a hole open at the back of it where it should have been up against the wall. It was hiding a room.

Three people jumped up nervously as we entered, two men and a woman. One man and the woman were not much older than me, but the other was much older, possibly in his seventies or eighties. "What's going on, Mendez?" he said nervously, looking up and down at our uniforms.

"Relax, they are friends," Mendez replied.

"Is there such a thing now?" the young woman asked contemptuously.

"Only if you want them," I responded.

"And what if we don't want them?" she said with snarky suspicion.

"Relax, Tiffany." The older man said with a surprisingly jovial tone. "Can't you see they are wearing the uniforms of the United States Marines? They are hardly going to be here to harm us."

"Nice to hear a voice of reason," I said, offering him my hand. "Lieutenant Dodgson. Pleased to meet you."

He took my hand and looked me up and down. "Have you never tried to fix that speech impediment of yours?"

This instantly took away my confidence. As I have already told you, I have not included references to my stammer in this text as it is a constant source of irritation to me and everyone else. However, on this occasion, it is rather important to mention. "It's not possible. It's been tried."

"Hmm! Impossible is not a word that I enjoy. However, now is not the time to discuss this. Doctor McKay, at your service. These are my two assistants, Atticus Blake and Tiffany Mahoney. Forgive Tiffany's attitude. She seems to have a corncob up her ass constantly."

Mahoney glared at him most viciously. Cearly, their relationship was not cordial. "Are you here to get us out ?" She said, turning back to me.

"Eventually, but we are in most need of your assistance," I replied.

"Ah, Lieutenant Dodgson, and here I was thinking we would get on so well." He chuckled. "You are after my technology, are you not? The new devices."

"Well, that too. However, all we know is that you've made some advances, but we do not know what exactly."

He smiled proudly, turned around to lift what looked like a small suitcase, and placed it on a table. I moved over to stand next to him and looked down as he opened it. Small flat cylindrical objects about two inches thick and the width of an outstretched palm were carefully placed in a foam casing. He looked at us proudly, but I just stared at him and shrugged. He rolled his eyes. "This is it. This is the new M.E.T.."

I looked at Pentauk, who also shrugged, and we both looked back at him and then back at the devices. He muttered something about the dumb military with a sigh. "These are the prototypes of a revolutionary portable M .E.T. system. Each can carry up to three personnel for two and a half hours."

My eyes widened. "The military applications of that are just phenomenal," I said.

"Not just military but intelligence and many other applications to get people into anywhere you want them to go."

"But why only two and a half hours?" I frowned.

"It requires a lot of power, and unfortunately, that is the best I can get a battery to maintain the charge for. When the battery dies, it can no longer maintain the energy pattern. Unfortunately, I was working on a way to release the inhabitants from the device automatically before that happened. But the surrender came, and I was unable to finish my work."

"Even so, that is an amazing accomplishment," Pentauk said.

He grinned at her with pride. But that grin dissipated when I said, "Admiral Plural will be exceedingly pleased with this."

He looked up at me, and his face had turned cold and angry. "You are with Jenna Plural?"

"Yes, Sir. We are part of the new Solar Confederation."

"Seriously?" he looked absolutely horrified. "Did you not hear that woman's speech? She is a fanatic." My face grew impassive as I glared at him. "She talks about the genocide of entire nations."

"She talks about freeing us from Peon tyranny," snapped Tiffany, throwing her hands in the air and turning away in frustration.

Atticus stepped up between them. "Look, let's calm this down. This really isn't the time to discuss politics."

"There is no way I am allowing my equipment to get into the hands of that psychopath," McKay shouted.

"I don't think you have an option," I said coldly.

He glared at me almost fanatically. "Oh, you think so." He spun around, grabbed a hammer, and swung it toward the box. But at the last second, he stiffened and dropped the hammer as I fired my snap pistol at him.

Tiffany squealed and jumped aside while Atticus placed his hands on either side of his head in disbelief. At my side, Pentauk muttered, "oh, fuck."

"What the hell are you doing!" Mendez cried out.

"I couldn't let him destroy that equipment," I said quite calmly. "It is too valuable to the war effort."

Tiffany recovered quite quickly, stating, "she had no choice. It's regrettable, but you were right. I heard Plural's speech too, and hell, I agree with her. Don't worry. I am sure I can finish his work."

"What are you going to do with us?" Atticus asked nervously.

"If you do not intend to stand in my way, I will get you out of here and back to the fleet," I replied.

"I wouldn't trust Atticus if I were you," Tiffany said coldly. "He's a complete toady to the doctor."

"You bitch!" Atticus stepped up to her, but I put my arm between them. "Back off."

A groan from the floor made us aware that the doctor was not dead. "Do you have a medic?" I said softly to Mendez

"No, but I know some basic first aid. Let me go get the kit."

I stepped over to the table and picked up one of the new devices feeling its weight in my hand. "How does this work?" I looked at Tiffany.

"Turn it on, place it on the floor, and get someone to stand over it." She replied.

I did exactly that, then looked at Atticus. "Get undressed."

But Tiffany smiled and said, "that is no longer necessary the individual can be uploaded clothed and with their equipment."

"Nice," I said, genuinely impressed. "Well, go on then. Stand over it." With a sigh of resignation, Atticus stepped over it and disappeared without the typical M.E.T. flash of light.

I looked up at Tiffany. "Your turn."

She raised her hands in protest. "Look, I understand that you may not trust me, but I assure you I'm on your side. There's no need to...."

I raised my own hand to stop her. "It's not about trust. I want to get you out of here alive. That will be easier if you're not running around as a potential target."

She sighed but reluctantly stood over their device. I looked down in amazement after she disappeared at the blinking light on the portable M.E.T.. I stepped over to it and picked it up. It had a small clip on the back, and I fastened it to the back of my belt and turned to Pentauk, who was just looking quite dazed about everything. "Come on, let's move out. We have an appointment with whoever thinks they are in charge here."

Chapter Eighteen

Taking Enceladus

T he monorail was a single track of dark energy powered pods that could hold six people. This bothered me somewhat since I could not take the whole team in one go. This became an even bigger concern when Amy said, "I'm only going to be able to get one of these pods going. We are on reduced power."

I looked back at Pentauk and said irritably, "pick four of your best and send the rest back to Mendez."

She nodded, and much to my annoyance, she chose Andreas amongst the four. Probably a good thing since it was necessary to watch one of them. "Leave your packs. Arms only."

I turned back to the pod. At least it was surrounded by glass, and we could get a complete view of our surroundings.

Amy seemed to take forever to complete her work, but she finally stood up and gave me a nod and a smile. "You're good to go!"

I turned back to Pentauk, gave her a nod, and watched my people get into the back.

I looked back at Amy. "Thank you, ma'am. You are going to be a valuable asset to the Confederation." She blushed lightly and nodded her gratitude without a word as I climbed into the front of the pod next to Pentauk.

Amy slid the door closed and slapped the roof. "Good luck!"

She then turned back to the panel she'd been working on, and with the press of a few buttons, we slid along into the tunnel. It was slower than I expected, failing to temper the nerves running through my body. Amy was in control, and we slid straight through various stops on the way to the central core.

There was a small electronic map of the network overhead, and I watched as we got closer to our destination. If security were alerted, we would be sitting ducks.

As we came within one stop of our destination, I started my weapons check, and my team followed suit. We were lucky. No one was waiting for us. I slipped my rifle over my shoulder and withdrew my officer's pistol as I climbed out first. We were in a small, clinically white reception area. There was a security desk, but no one was seated at it. Clearly, our opponents were not professional.

Silently I pointed at two of my people and then at either side of the door. I nodded to the technician to move forward and check the door locks. He pulled some gizmo from his belt and attached it to the door. We waited while the small device buzzed, then he pulled it off and looked back at me with a nod before dashing back behind me.

214

I nodded to one of the regular marines, and she stepped forward and hit the opening. The door slid open, and the gunfire began. I dived for cover as bullets rained over my head. Before I even got up, my team was returning fire. It had at first seemed as if there were many opponents, but there were only two. They were dressed in civilian security uniforms and didn't stand a chance against battle-hardened United States Marines. They were dead within seconds. I stepped into the corridor and stuck a bullet into each head with my snap pistol just to make sure. I glanced back at my team. "Any injuries?" That was a negative, and I moved forward into the long corridor to another door.

"Well, there it goes, our element of surprise," Pentauk said.

I did not reply and nodded to the next door, and the process was repeated. This time I stood further back behind the door. When no fire came, a marine moved around the door, raised his rifle, and stepped in. "No sudden moves," he shouted. "Keep your hands in the air where I can see them." One by one, my people filed in, and I brought up the rear.

We were in a large operation center with dozens of people who looked like they were civilians. There was fear on their faces which meant we had control. There were three rows of desks with computer screens looking reminiscent of an astrodome flight control. "Nice and easy everyone, and no one gets hurt," Pentauk instructed.

I holstered my pistol, stepped up to the center of the room, and stood with my hands behind my back. "Who is in charge here?" I asked, but no one answered. I sighed and repeated myself more curtly. "Who is in charge here?"

"We are American citizens," An older woman said indignantly, looking at me quite aggressively, albeit with her hands raised high. "You have no right to do this."

"In that case, you have nothing to worry about, do you, madam?" I replied coldly. "However you failed to respond to the lawful communications of fleet Admiral Jenna Plural. That warrants an immediate investigation."

"Jenna Plural does not represent the American government," a young man shouted at me. "She is a nutjob fascist renegade." I heard the hatred in his speech. "She's some weird fanatic."

I fixed my eyes on the young man who had just spoken to me. "The Solar Confederation is now responsible for the welfare of all free people and American territory that is not in the hands of the European Union. That includes this base. Anyone who does not recognize that will be considered to be committing treason."

"But that makes no sense. The President is the authority." It was the old lady again.

"In surrendering, the President declared herself a traitor to the American people. We no longer recognize the authority of the Earth-based government, which is now a puppet of the Peons." I said, trying desperately to temper my anger and not have everyone here executed on the spot.

"So you expect us to follow that right-wing fanatic," the young man snapped back.

I had enough of this, and to the horror of all around, including, I believe, a couple of my people, I pulled out my snap pistol and shot him in the head. As his brain matter flew out the back of his head and he fell across his desk, panic started to rise within our prisoners.

"Stay where you are. Nobody move," Pentauk shouted, and my guys stood in front of the two other exits to ensure no one made it to the door. I waited patiently for order to be restored. I then said quite coldly, "does anyone else have a problem with the authority of Admiral Jenna Plural?"

No one did. There was an old saying, I can't remember who said it, and it's quite crude, but it was very apt to our situation. 'When you've got them by the balls, their hearts and minds will follow." I had them by the balls.

"I will ask this only one more time," I said in my most pleasant tone. "Who is in charge here?" again, a long silence followed until someone plucked up the courage to say. "You just shot him, ma'am."

I sighed softly, "well, who's next in line then? You are seriously trying my patience here."

"I am," replied the older woman but with a lot less cocky tone now.

"Name?"

"Catherine Marsters ."

"Well, Catherine Marsters, you will sit down nicely with Seargeant Pentauk here and give her a full list of your personnel and security setup. You will instruct all your security forces to disarm and find a decent place where my people can process them. If all goes well, further violence will not be needed." At this point, I was startled to hear the door down the corridor we had entered open. As we spun around, we saw that it was another six members of our team. Good old Amy. This would make things easier.

I looked up at the corporal leading them. "Find somewhere we can hold the prisoners. Get a full list of names and occupations."

He nodded and headed out as I turned back to the civilians, "In a moment, Corporal Lincoln will be taking you out of here. Behave nicely for him, and nothing will happen to you. However, I want your communication specialist and your environment and life specialist." After a moment's hesitation, a young girl stepped forward. She barely looked old enough to vote. She raised her hand nervously. "I am the communication specialist."

"Name?" I asked.

"Liz Nolan."

"Well, Miss Nolan, take a seat at your station but don't touch anything." She nodded and complied. I looked around the room, waiting for the other person to own up. "It's been a long day, and I am very tired. I am usually a very patient person. I will ask for the last time. Who is the environment and life officer?"

A young woman elbowed the man at her side, and reluctantly he stepped forward. "I am miss. Brandon Meyer."

I nodded to him. "Take your place, Brandon, and again don't touch anything."

The corporal returned and advised me that he'd found somewhere, and with a nod from me, he led everyone out except for the three I had held back.

"Okay, Brandon, I want you to give me a list of everyone in this base."

He looked at me, confused. "I can surely do that, ma'am, but there are thousands of people here." Behind me, I heard Andreas give a loud contemptuous snort at my expense. I felt the heat of embarrassment rising within me but said. "If you let me finish, Brandon. I want a list of everyone armed."

"I can give you a list of people who are authorized to be armed, but I can't detect weaponry from here."

"Just do it, Brandon. You're starting to annoy me." I snapped. However, my stammer made it barely audible, but he understood.

"Yes, ma'am," he replied.

I stepped over to Liz. "Patch me into the Confederation fleet." I gave her the frequencies and the codes required. Her hands darted over her keyboard until a voice echoed throughout the room. "We are reading you, Dodgson." He knew who we were by the codes I had given. "The Admiral was asked to put us you straight through to her. Please hold the line."

There was a short pause before Admiral Plural's voice came back, "Good to hear from you, Dodgson. Report."

"Ma'am, we have control over the Enceladus Base," I replied.

"Understood." Her tone was intense and less pleased than I was expecting. What she said next gave me my answer as to why. "I am sorry to tell you that you have the Peon fleet closing in on your location. I don't know if they know what you're doing or if it's just bad timing. I have ordered the fleet to intercept them, but we will not be there before they reach you. What's the situation on the weapon systems?"

"Give me a moment to confer with our personnel here, and I will let you know," I replied.

"Go for it," she replied.

I looked over at Brandon. "Give me a sitrep of the weapon systems of this base."

"All weapon systems offline to conserve power," he replied uneasily. I assume he was concerned about my reaction to this bad news.

"How long will it take you to bring them back online.?"

He hesitated before replying, "I can't. At least not from here. They were manually disabled at the source."

I must admit to my shame that I actually swore. "Did you hear that, Admiral Plural?" I asked her.

"I did." There was a pause before, very carefully, she said, "Dodgson. If you don't get those weapons online, the Peons will get a foothold on Enceladus, and we won't have a hope in hell of taking that base or even picking you up."

"Don't worry, ma'am. If there's a way to get them online, we will do it."

"That's my girl. Let me know how you get on, Plural out." A chill of excitement ran up my spine as she called me *her* girl. I was *not* going to let her down.

Enceladus Base had four primary guns that fired dumb fire missiles. Naturally, this took quite a bit of power, but even so, it would not have been the first thing I would have powered down even if peace had been declared.

It should not have been that problematic. A simple monorail ride to each emplacement, but things are never quite that easy, are they?

I had with me my tech and just two of my people. I wasn't expecting a problem. We sweep in, reactivate the gun, and get out.

The pod took us into the weapon control center. Of course, we could not just walk in there. I required the tech back at the environmental life station to unseal the doors. It then took my guy less than four minutes to bring the massive cannon back online.

We repeated the process with the second, but everything went wrong while we were on our way to the third. We were zipping along with the monorail when the faint hum of its DE engine suddenly cut out. I tensed and looked about as I gripped my snap pistol in its holster. We gradually began to slow down and eventually stopped. The on-board computer spoke to us in soft, reassuring tones that didn't in the least reassure me. "Please stay calm. We are suffering a power outage. Maintenance drones have been dispatched, and we will be underway as soon as possible."

I pulled up my comlink, "Pentauk, what is going on?"

"Can't talk. We're under attack," she came back, and I could hear the sound of rapid gunfire in the background.

"Holy moly," I muttered. I turned to see if the door could open, but it was sealed shut to stop the civilians from doing exactly what I was trying to do.

I turned to Baxter, the tech. "Can you do anything?"

"I can but try." He said cheerfully and climbed out of his seat and over the other two at the back until he was at the rear of the pod. He pulled out some doohickey and ran it along on a panel. I got back on the radio. "Pentauk report."

"They got us pinned down in the control center," she replied. "Station security decided not to comply with your instructions, ma'am."

"How are you holding up?"

"I have lost three, but we have taken out more of them than they have of us," she shouted.

"Do you think you can deal with that while we carry on with our mission, or do we need to return?" I asked calmly.

"You can carry on, ma'am. Leave this to us."

As the line went dead, I looked back at Baxter. "How's it going back there."

"Just another minute, ma'am." He replied.

"Make it forty seconds." I snapped.

"Ma'am, if I say it will take him a minute, it will take a minute," he told me.

"Hey, I was just saying what they say in the movies. Carry on." I shrugged.

He chuckled just as the door to the pod slid open. I jumped out, followed by my team, with Baxter bringing up the rear. I looked up and down the gleaming white tube, wondering whether it was best to go ahead or back. Having already visited two of the weapon sites, we were probably the furthest from Pentauk we could get. "Let's move on. Keep weapons ready and be prepared for anything. "

We moved off down the tunnel, unaware of how long it would take us, as I did not know the speed with which we were traveling in that tube. After a few minutes, I radioed Pentauk again. "Sitrep?"

"They have thrown everything they have at us, but we're holding our own." Came the reply amid the gunfire.

"Casualties?"

"I have six down." As she said this, we came out by a monorail station. Not the one we wanted, but I decided then and there that it would probably be quicker if we cut through the base.

However, as we climbed onto the platform, I heard a bullet whizz past my head. There was a cry behind me, but I was already firing at the security officer who had come out of the doorway. Behind me, two other rifles opened up, bringing him down in a hail of bullets. As I turned back to my team, I looked down with frustration at the dead body of our tech. "Take off his equipment belt. We have to keep moving." I instructed one of the troopers. "Helen is going to be miffed," I muttered.

"Ma'am, this stuff is useless without someone who knows how to use it." One replied to me.

"We can worry about that once we get there. Come on, let's move out." The three of us went through the doorway that the security guard had come through. Very slowly and cautiously.

It was not like I knew the way to the next gun. I knew it was on the outer ring, and if we kept to the outer edge of the base, we would come to it eventually. However, barely fifteen minutes later, our progress stopped at the end of the corridor, a sealed door. With no Baxter or Andreas, it looked like we would have to retrace our steps and find another route until something occurred to me. I reached the back of my belt and pulled off the small M.E.T. device.

I studied it carefully until I was confident about the recall switch. I clicked it and placed the disc on the ground as it began a countdown from ten to zero. It did not give me an option on who to get out of the device, but as I would later find out, it released people in reverse order. The last one in was the first one out, and I was pleased to see that it was Tiffany Mahoney that appeared in front of me. "How long?" was the first thing she asked.

"Just a couple of hours," I replied. "We thought we had control of the base, but the station security has launched a counterattack on the control center. We have a Peon fleet headed our way, and I'm trying to get the guns back online while my number one is trying to maintain control of operations. I've lost my technician, and I need your help."

Tiffany nodded. "What can I do?"

"For a start, you can get that door open."

At that, she simply smiled, turned around, and punched in some numbers on a keypad by the door, and it slid open. I muttered a curse to myself as I realized that had I left her out of the M.E.T., she could have legitimately opened every door I required.

We continued on our way, keeping Tiffany behind me but in front of the other two for her safety. We carried on for almost thirty minutes, alert for signs of danger. I was growing tired and frustrated. However, Pentauk finally called me with some good news. "We have secured the control center, Lieutenant."

"Very good. Casualties?

"I'm sorry to say we lost seven, ma'am."

"Understood. Maintain vigilance and carry on." As the line went dead, I found we had arrived at the doorway of the third gun. Tiffany opened the door, and at my instruction, she brought it up online. As we heard the massive gun grind into position, slipping out of the base's dome to point upwards, Pentauk came online again. "Lieutenant, we have started picking up ships on our scanners' outer edge. ETA about twenty minutes until they're in range of our guns. "

"Understood. As soon as they are in range, you can start firing. Try to identify their command ships and make them the primary targets."

In range was a loose term when fighting in space, for there was no maximum distance you could fire at something. With no resistance, a missile could carry on forever. When we use the term in range, we refer simply to the least amount of time they have to respond. The further away a ship was, the more time it had to maneuver out of its way.

I was surprised we did not run into anyone as we continued onwards. It was only afterward I found out that our opponents in the base had locked everyone down, having everyone remain in their quarters as they tried to deal with us.

Just as we were managing to power up the final gun, a base-wide communication came online. A thick Texan-accented voice boomed out. "This is Edward Granger, the official voice of the Science Quorum. I am talking to the commander of the American forces currently acting against us. We do not recognize your authority here. This base has declared itself an independent state. We do not want to escalate the situation, but if you don't surrender now, we will activate the internal automated weapon systems and deactivate your marine pin safety protocols. I give you five minutes to respond."

As the final gun moved into position, I looked around for an intercom. Finding one on the wall, I stepped up to it and hit the button. "This base is now the official territory of the Solar Confederation under Admiral Jenna Plural. Do you really think that they won't just send more if you take us out?"

The reply came with a haughty laugh. "Well, now that you have reactivated the external weaponry, any of your ships coming into range can be fired upon. However, it is not my wish to make an enemy of anyone. That's why I'm giving you this chance to do the right thing and stand down."

"I don't know if you have access to long-range scanners," I responded. "But a Peon fleet is coming here to question your authority to remain in control of your base. You pretty much have two alternatives. One is to join us. The other is to accept yourself as a puppet state of the European imperium."

There was this long silent pause before he replied, "You appear to be right on that. I am willing to discuss terms with you."

"Have all your people stand down and not resist us. Where do you want to meet." I demanded.

"I don't think it's necessary for us to meet in person. We can continue our conversation over the intercoms."

"So, you want us to leave you out there so you can change your mind once we have dealt with the Peons?" I said snarkily.

"That's about the size of it," he replied. "What you are suggesting is I turn myself over to either you or the Peons to what could potentially be a long term of imprisonment or execution."

"That's not for me to judge. I'm not law enforcement, and your ultimate fate is not mine to decide unless, of course, you continue fighting us." I paused and then continued, "honestly, all I care about is securing this base and making sure it doesn't fall into the hands of the enemy. It will be Admiral Plural who ultimately decides the fate of everyone in this station. I can assure you, Sir, that she is most fair and equitable. And by cooperate, I mean fully and completely."

"I see I'm not going to have a lot of choice in this." Another sigh and another pause. "Very well. I will meet you in the control center with a small complement of personal security."

"No. Bring anyone armed, and we will shoot you on sight. Am I understood?" I stated firmly.

"You are basically asking me to surrender myself to you," he said incredulously.

"All I am asking you is to discontinue being a threat to us, nothing more and nothing less. Do you agree or don't you? I have no more time to waste in this banter."

Again another irritating pause before he replied, "Very well, I will see you in thirty minutes."

"One last thing before you go. Was it you who disabled the monorail?"

"It was."

"I would appreciate it if you would reactivate it."

Chapter Nineteen

The Peons are Coming

Back in the Control center, it was a mess. Pentauk was arranging the removal of the bodies, and several consoles were smoking from gunfire damage. The environment and life officer lay slumped over the console, his head to one side, his eyes staring at me lifelessly. I nodded to one of the marines, and he pulled the man from the seat as I turned to Tiffany. "Can you handle the environment and life systems?"

She shrugged. "I don't see why not." She stepped up to the console, looked down at the blood-splattered keyboard, and then looked at me in disgust.

I just shrugged. "We all have to make do, ma'am."

She flopped into the seat with clear irritation, and with the last look at the keyboard and a disgusted sigh, she started tapping away.

I spun about as the door opened, and a small, portly, balding man stood in the doorway, raising his hands uneasily as he faced our raised weapons. "Edward Granger. You are expecting me." He was wearing an expensive business suit, and at his side was a tall young woman dressed in a feminine version of the same outfit with a knee-length skirt. She stood slightly behind him, and I correctly assessed that she was his personal assistant.

"Come in, Mr. Granger." I said curtly. "but keep your hands where we can see them until you've been searched." He complied quite calmly, not showing any concern about his current situation. One of my marines went over and frisked him first and then the woman at his side.

"This is my personal assistant, Miss Crystal Garrett." He introduced her even though I didn't care. She was a thin-lipped officious-looking woman who did not appear to be as at ease as her boss. She looked around each of my people with stern concern.

"I assume you are head of the criminal cartel that is operating here," I asked Granger.

"That is quite an assumption, Lieutenant," Garrett said quite coldly.

"Fine, if you want to play games, then this conversation is not going to go anywhere." I turned away, waving my hand dismissively at them. "You are clearly no science quorum."

"I'm only pointing out that Mr. Granger has never been accused of any crime in his entire life and that doing so will incur serious repercussions." Garret fixed her steely gaze upon me.

"Really?" I could not help but grin as I turned back to them. "Repercussions with who exactly?"

The confidence in her face dissipated quickly. "well. I...."

"Oh, I think we can dispense with the legalities of everything, Crystal. I think Lieutenant..." he looked down at the name on my chest, "Dodgson is fully aware of what we are and who we are. We are all effectively outside of any governmental rule at present."

"On the contrary, you are now subject to the authority of the Solar Confederation," I said curtly. "However, you should be aware that any constitutional rights you may have had as a United States citizen no longer apply. A state of martial law is in effect. And that, sir, gives me a wide latitude to respond as someone appropriate."

"That sounds like a threat, Lieutenant." The man replied uneasily.

"I'm just informing you of your rights," I replied, then added with a shrug, "or rather, the lack of them." I then turned away and walked over to the communications officer. She looked nervous and was shaking a little, and she had signs that she had been crying. "Open up communications to the fleet."

She looked up at me. "Which one?"

"Ours, of course," I responded irritably.

She tapped a few buttons, and the communications officer on board the USS constitution put me straight through to the Admiral. "Good to hear your voice again, Dodgson. How's it going down there?"

"I must admit I had a brief loss of control, and we lost six people." I knew better than not to tell the truth of the matter. "A criminal cartel has unofficially run this place. However, the leader has turned himself over to us."

"Well, that's not exactly how I would put it," said Granger. "My understanding is I am here under a flag of truce, not as a prisoner."

"Switch to visual communications." The Admiral instructed, and the communications officer complied without waiting for me to give the order. The beautiful and graceful face of Admiral Jenna Plural appeared on the screen in large high-definition perfection. Judging from the background, she was clearly in her quarters and had her jacket off, indicating that she was off duty when I called. "I am Jenna Plural, fleet Admiral of the Solar Confederation. Who do I have the honor of addressing?"

"Edward Granger, chief executive of Enceladus Projects Incorporated."

"I thought so when I heard your voice. Well, Mr. Granger, I hope you are being cooperative with Lieutenant Dodgson, but I need to be assured. Be honest with me. I will know if you're lying. Where do your loyalties lie."

"My loyalties lie squarely with Enceladus Projects Incorporated. I am unconcerned about who is in government, but I'd rather not be subject to the European Union under the current circumstances."

Admiral Plural smiled. "Well, that is more honest than I expected." She sat back and folded her arms. "However, it would be more honest if you said you are a member of the New York Fraternity."

His eyes widened. "How very astute of you."

She chuckled lightly at this. "Not really, Mr. Granger. You do not recall it, but we have met. That is why I had my colleague turn on the camera so I could be sure." She called me 'colleague.' My heart skipped a beat!

"I can assure you that had I met you. I would remember such a beautiful woman as yourself!" Granger said smarmily.

"Oh, this was over thirty years ago, so maybe not." Jenna sat back in her chair and relaxed.

Granger grinned. "Ah, so the rumor is true. You are a GenMod Miss Plural."

The Admiral's eyes narrowed. "I don't like that term, Mr. Granger. Please do not let me hear you use it again. And it is Admiral Plural, if you please, not 'Miss.'"

"Apologies, my dear lady. Yet I still do not recall you." Granger's smile did not falter.

"You saved the life of my associate Rockford Harlow."

The realization suddenly came to him. "Oh my, you are Jenn? If I recall, you were more than his associate. How is the old bastard? He must be knocking on eighty by now."

"He died at the Battle of Deep Space." The was a hint of remorse in her voice. I admit I was surprised, I had met Harlow on The Chesty, but I would never have imagined he was that close to the Admiral.

"I'm sorry to hear that. He was a good guy," Granger said reflectively.

"That he was, but he regretted not being able to bring your gang down. However, the only reason I'm talking to you and not having you arrested is because of Rocky. Cooperate fully with Dodgson, and there may possibly be a role for your organization as we move forward."

Granger looked quite surprised and raised a grey eyebrow. "You are willing to do business with us."

"I assume you can negotiate on behalf of the entire cartel?"

"You assume correctly, Admiral Plural. I hold the rank of Senior Brother, and my word will be honored by all sections of our community."

"Very well. Assuming we do not lose Enceladus to the Peons, I believe we can do business." With that, she turned her attention back to me. "How goes the situation with the base's defenses?"

"All weaponry is now online. We have four dumb fire cannons ready and waiting." I informed her.

"Good, that's great to hear." The Admiral smiled. "We are on our way there as fast as possible, but you may have to hold out for a while before we can get to you." She was about to sign off when something occurred to her. "There is one other thing, Dodgson. We have lost contact with Captain Grant and Mr. Phelkar. Her last communication was that she was under attack. We have no idea where she is now. Do you know anything?"

"No, ma'am. I saw her leave. She showed no signs of distress." I replied.

The admiral sighed. "Okay, Dodgson, keep up the good work. Plural out."

"We are receiving communication from a European ship," Liz Nolan said, looking up at me from her seat.

"What are they saying?" I asked impatiently.

"They are saying they are landing with the authority of the United States government," She responded.

I could not help but grin at this. They weren't attacking. They were moving in with United States authority to take control. They expected to simply land and take over.

I turned to Tiffany. "Can you set the weapons to open fire when the first ships are in the moon's gravitational pull?

"Not a problem," she said with a tone of voice which meant, 'yeah, give me something hard to do, would you?'"

Then Pentauk came up to my side, looking concerned. "Isn't that cutting it a bit fine, Lieutenant?"

I turned to her, my face grinning like the Cheshire Cat from my favorite childhood story. "Don't you see? They think they will come in as if we are happily capitulating to them. The closer we let them get, the more ships there will be in range." Pentauk nodded but still looked unsure. "Trust me," I said softly.

She nodded again and moved away from me. I knew I did not have her trust and still had to earn it.

However, on the scanner, I saw the Peons begin to slow down, keeping back, and I frowned, wondering what the problem was.

"You didn't respond to their hails," Tiffany said as if reading my mind. "Not hearing from you is making them nervous."

"But I don't speak French!" I replied.

Tiffany rolled her eyes. "They sure make marines dumb, don't they? This is an American base, and they *know* it's an American base. They won't expect you to be speaking damn French, stupid. They will expect you to respond in

English, though. You can speak English, can't you, Lieutenant?"

I felt myself flush as I turned back to the communications officer and told them to open an audio-only line to the French fleet. "This is Dodgson. Sorry for the delay in responding, but I'm sure you understand we were quite nervous seeing a European fleet coming toward us."

I was surprised when an American voice came back to me. "No worries, Miss Dobson. This is Captain Peter Lane representing the provisional government of the United States. We are working with European High Command on the peaceful transition to the new situation."

"Understood, Captain Lane. Can I be assured that no one here will be harmed?"

"As long as no one resists European authority over the base, I can assure you no one will be harmed."

"It's going to be great to go home. We will prepare the landing ports for you," I said cheerfully.

"I'm looking forward to meeting you, Miss Dobson." He said merrily, causing my stomach to twist inside. He was a damn traitor, and no one could doubt that. "It's Dodgson," I muttered as he went offline

"That was odd!" Pentauk said softly at my side.

I glanced at her. "What was?

"An American in command of a French vessel."

"Oh, I am sure he's not in charge. He is just a voice for the damn Peons. They think it's more likely that we would comply with an American than the enemy."

"So what now?" She asked.

"We make it look like we're getting ready for them to land and prepare the ports." I turned to Granger. "Can I trust you to see to that?"

He smiled and turned to Crystal. "See to that, would you, my dear."

"Of course, Sir." She walked to the door to leave but faced one of my men. She looked back at me. "With your permission, of course, Lieutenant," she said icily.

"Let her through, Baker," I said with a grin, and the marine stepped aside. As she left, I turned around and sat in the seat next to the communications officer.

"And just what are we going to be doing?" Granger asked.

"We are going to wait. Situation report, please, Tiffany."

This time Tiffany smiled. "I am pleased to report that the ships are once more moving toward us. Weapons powered down."

I heard a faint beeping and looked around. But I couldn't tell where it was coming from. I tried to ignore it. "How long before they come within the range I specified?"

"About another thirty minutes."

The beeping behind me got louder and suddenly became a long, ongoing tone. I stood up and turned around. But still, the sound came from behind me. "What is that annoying noise?"

"Oh, that's the portable M.E.T.," Tiffany said casually, not even looking over from her console, where she continued to monitor the progress of the Peons. "It was warning you that the power was low. Not bad going because it's been nearly three hours. Much longer than expected."

I quickly pulled the M.E.T. device from the back of my belt. It was indeed where the tone was coming from.

I looked up at Tiffany, confused. "You said 'was'?"

Tiffany shrugged and smiled slightly. "The long tone means the contents have lost coherence."

I looked down at the device and then back up at her. "Are you telling me that he's dead?"

"Absolutely." She replied quite chirpily.

"Why didn't you tell me?" I responded, aghast.

Tiffany sounded bored as she shrugged again. "Honestly, I did not want him to come out. And also, to be equally honest, he wouldn't cooperate with Jenna Plural. He was a pathetic little man who always whined on about the morality of our research being used for warfare."

"That was not your call. It was mine. I should have you arrested," I said angrily.

"Pfft!" She turned to me and rolled her eyes lazily, saying, "I am far too valuable to be wasted in a jail cell. Your Jenna Plural will want more of these devices and have me develop them further. Also, I hate to be pedantic, but it was not my responsibility to inform you about it. We already told you the battery only lasts two hours."

I tossed the device to Pentauk. "See if you can find somewhere to charge that. We may need to use it again for someone else." I looked back at Tiffany as I said the last part, and she shot me a startled look.

"I can assure you, Lieutenant. It is the right decision. With the doctor's research, there is no end to the possibilities I can deliver. He would have just continued to cause problems."

I sighed, aware that she was probably right but not liking the situation all the same.

I sat down in a chair and closed my eyes. It was only then that I thought about what happened to Stacey Grant. Mr. Phelkar was with her, and a knot tightened in my stomach. I would make her pay dearly if she had let anything happen to him.

"Hold onto your seats, everyone." Tiffany's shout drew me from my thoughts. I opened my eyes and looked over at her. "The first ship is coming into range in thirty seconds. Our weapons are powering up."

"Is there any way we can get it on the screen," I asked urgently

Tiffany shook her head. "Nope, it's not like we have cameras looking out into space."

"What's happening?

"Our first gun is preparing to fire." And then there was a sudden boom from somewhere far within the base, and Tiffany punched the air. "Direct hit into the underbelly of the beast. The first ship is going down. The other ships are starting to raise their maneuver, but...." Before she could finish her sentence, two more guns bellowed out, closely followed by the third. "Three more direct hits. We have taken out three cruisers." Tiffany laughed. "The other ships are starting to pull up and backing away but not fast enough."

The guns boomed out again. This time three hits on a miss.

"The Peon ship is calling us again." Said Nolan.

"Put them on speaker," I commanded.

"What the hell is going on down there," Captain Lane shouted. "If you don't stop at once, they will order that entire decimation of that base."

"Oh no, you won't," I replied cheerily. "You know full well you have orders to get the research from this base. You don't want to destroy it."

"What do you hope to achieve, girl? If we need to, we can just sit back and wait until your supplies run out because nothing is coming here from Earth anymore, you stupid bitch."

"Sir, you are talking to an officer of the Solar Confederation. This base is under the direct command of Admiral Jenna Plural. I advise you to turn around and retreat. You are within our territory, and we will take no prisoners."

"Jenna Plural?" Lane positively spluttered out her name. "She is a damn delusional lieutenant. You are mad to be throwing in with her."

"We have already taken out almost half their ships," Tiffany called over to me. "However they have moved sufficiently far away that they are not having a problem avoiding our dumb fire missiles."

"Stop the firing. No point in wasting missiles," I commanded, and the guns fell silent. "Captain, as you and your Peon masters can see, you haven't a hope in heck of getting near us."

"The union wants this base," he responded. "And is willing to wait for it. When was your last supply run? Where is this fucking Jenna Plural? Is she going ride over the horizon and rescue you?" " He suddenly stopped talking as someone said something to him. He made some blasphemous curses and then cut the line.

"Lieutenant," Tiffany called over to me, and I turned to face her. "The Peon ships are heading out at a very strange trajectory from the moon. It looks like they're leaving." I stepped over to her and looked at the scanner. And then, right on the edge, a blip appeared. The USS Constitution was still several hours out but at the head of the entire fleet. "And she is coming up over the horizon." I laughed and slapped Tiffany on the back.

CHAPTER TWENTY

WINS AND LOSSES

The celebrations for taking the Enceladus Base rivaled those for the Battle of Deep Space. The big difference was it took place on the ground. Solid ground that many in the fleet had not stood upon in months or even years.

Several ships came down and landed with a complement of troops and technicians who secured the base. Pentauk and I went down to the docking bay where Jenna Plural's shuttle landed. There was quite a crowd gathered, all desperate to see the woman who had saved them. As she came down the shuttle ramp, I noticed she looked over to where I now saw the Jezebel Stacey Grant standing, and I immediately looked around to see if I could see Mr. Phelkar, but there was no sign of him. Grant looked seriously messed up. Her face was black and blue and severely swollen. She had been through the wringer. She probably deserved it.

Admiral Plural made her way over to her, and they spoke very briefly before the Admiral turned away and headed back toward me. I glared at the Jezebel, but she did not appear to notice me and just turned away, heading back to her shuttle.

Just before she reached me, I saw Admiral Plurals wipe something from her eye, but then she smiled at me. "Quite an amazing job you've done there, Lieutenant Dodgson." She o returned my salute and then put out our hand to shake mine.

As we walked up to the control center, I told her the story of what had happened. She let some civilians come into the room and addressed all present. "This is another victory for the infant Solar Confederation, taking us one step closer back to Earth. Enceladus is the first of what will be many bases and colonies loyal to the cause of freedom. Let this be our capital at the beacon of hope to those who hide in terror from their oppressors. To victory!" she raised a defiant fist in the air, and the cry to victory went up from all around.

When Admiral Plural learned about the M.E.T. equipment, Tiffany was immediately offered a position in Helen Tracker's team and shipped out to the Constitution. Mendes and Amy were offered positions on board the fleet. Mendez chose to remain on Enceladus, but Amy accepted. Dr. McKay did not survive his wounds. It did not matter as we already had all we needed from him, and it was clear he would never have cooperated. It appeared Tiffany's wish to get credit for everything was going to come true. I, however, was not going to get the gratitude that I believe I deserved, for as we returned to the USS Constitution on board a transport shuttle, Pentauk came and sat next to me. She looked a little uncomfortable before saying to me, "you said that after this mission, we could decide whether to remain under your command or not."

I looked at her, disappointed. "From your tone, I am guessing you have decided that you will not be."

"Yes. We feel you got lucky." She said, discomfort at having to say it in her tone. "We do not feel safe or secure under your command."

I felt sick. "I gave you a choice, and the commodore agreed." I shrugged but inside, I was in turmoil. The mission was darn successful, the heck's sake. Ungrateful little poopheads.

Pentauk went to say something more, but I raised my hand and shook my head. She sighed, rose from her chair went back to her seat.

I looked ahead where the pilots sat, unable to look any of them in the eye. And when we landed, I remained in that position until they had all disembarked. I only came out when I was sure they would be clear of the docking area.

The news that Stacey Grant had allowed Mr. Phelkar to be captured by the Peons distracted me from my negative thoughts about myself and moved them squarely toward her. Given what she recently wrote in that debauched chronicle "That Girl from Wagga," you may think I am unfair in my vehemence. However, he was a civilian. Thus it was her responsibility to keep him safe. She failed and failed abysmally. This is what comes of relying on foreign help. The darn Australians had already proved they did not have what it takes to win a war.

When the news came that Stacey's sister had directly betrayed us, I knew it was more than a coincidence. There was a traitor in our midst, and it was clearly Stacefield Ellen Grant. She admitted it as much when she renamed the USS Los Angeles to the RAS Wagga Wagga. The Solar Confederation was American, and Jenna had said nothing about giving that up. Grant defamed the name of a fine ship by naming it after some outback Australian shantytown.

There was only one thing to do, but I didn't have the opportunity to do it. She was safely ensconced aboard the Los Angeles. Yes, I'm not going to call it by that pathetic name *she* gave it. I was aboard the Constitution.

I had no current duty. Commodore Addison put me on administrative leave without prejudice when she learned of my team's decision. She had questioned me long about it. She did not understand why after my great success, my team still wished to depart my unit. But the result was that I was without a portfolio.

Even my relationship with Helen Tracker seemed to have gone sour. She was always working and never had time for me.

One morning a couple of weeks later, I received a call to go to Admiral Plural's office,

"Hey, Dodgson." She said with a smile as I entered. She sat back in her chair, returning my salute without getting up. "I'm sorry that it's taken this long for me to get in touch with you, but I only just learned what happened after your mission. I can't say I'm happy with you for giving them that choice, but I'm not going to leave you dangling in the wind any longer. At the insistence of my security, I'm putting together a personal bodyguard of people I trust. Sakamoto will be in charge of that, and I want you and Abigail Thompson to join that team. Your basic job will be to keep me alive."

"That would be quite an honor, and ma'am, thank you for having faith in me." Although the idea of taking orders from a Jap did not sit well with me.

"Yes, well, I don't think it's unnecessary, but apparently, it's expected." The Admiral said, clearly irritated at the idea. "You will only be called to duty when I leave the Constitution. I will return you to logistics work when you aren't performing that duty. It really is a civilian role, but I want you to fill it until I find someone suitable to take over permanently."

"I take it there's no possibility of getting Mr. Phelkar back," I asked.

At this, she sighed and looked away from me, staring off into space for a moment before looking back at me. "Unfortunately, not Dodgson. You are dismissed."

I spent a couple of days settling into a new office and handling issues of the civilian craft. There was a need to transfer some supplies between the Constitution and the Los Angeles stop. I took the opportunity to oversee that operation personally using the excuse I wanted to perform an inspection of my staff.

I took a shuttle over to the Los Angeles and left my people dealing with whatever they had to deal with, for, to be honest, I wasn't there for any inspection. I headed up toward the bridge. I didn't know how I was going to do it, and clearly, I was going to get caught doing it, but I knew it was necessary. I was surprised that I got all the way to the bridge without anyone questioning me, and I found myself standing outside Stacey Grant's quarters. I do not know how I knew she was in there. This was a darn big ship, and she could be anywhere, but I just knew she was behind that door.

I could not believe the opportunity had come so easily. My heart raced as I stepped into her quarters. To rid the world of that foul creature, Stacey Grant, would be a joy to experience. However, she was not there. I looked about and was about to give up and leave when I heard a gentle sobbing from the bathroom. I opened it, and there she was, leaning her hands against the sink with her back to me. Making sure I did not step into view of the mirror. I withdrew my knife. Her body convulsed slightly as she continued to sob. It would be quick and clean and straight across her throat. She would barely feel it.

Yes, I know I am soft; I should have let her suffer with pain and indignity for her sins, but as I got closer, my eyes dropped to the small sliver of plastic lying on the counter. My eyes widened, and I hesitated. Then took a step back, quickly slipping the knife back into my belt. There in front of me was a pregnancy test with a thin pink line showing positive. Stacey suddenly turned around and jumped with a gasp as she saw me. "What the fuck, Dodgson?" She snapped at me while she wiped the tears from her eyes. She quickly grabbed the pregnancy test and tossed it into the garbage can. "You don't just walk into a girl in the dunny."

"I'm sorry, ma'am. I heard you, and I thought you were in some sort of distress."

She stared at me and said, "what the fuck do you want, Dodgson?

I can't remember the excuse I made, but she either appeared to accept it or was too wrapped up in her concerns to care. She glanced toward the garbage can and then slowly looked back at me, "I don't know what you saw there or even if you did, but it's private." she said venomously. "Tell anyone, and you and I will have a *real* big problem. Are you hearing me, Emma?"

"Understood, ma'am," I replied as I tried to make sense of all this.

"Good. Now fuck off." She waved her hand dismissively at me.

I nodded, turned to leave, and as I headed out, I felt so confused. However, by the time I made it back to my quarters, everything was so very clear. That time Jenna had made sweet love to me, I had become pregnant. However, Stacey Grant was the vessel to carry our child. As I got a coffee from the machine, I sat back in the chair with a huge grin.

For now, I know the truth. It is all so very clear.

Jenna Plural is God in human form.

Judgement Day is coming, and the power of Jenna will descend upon the sinners, and in her wrath, the galaxy will burn. Our child will rise, and whoever has crossed me will kneel before him and repent but all too late. Oh, how glorious it would be.

Hallelujah.

EPILOGUE

BY MICHAEL PHELKAR, FIRST MINISTER OF CIVIL AFFAIRS

Lieutenant Emma Susan Dodgson died less than a year after the end of the events she chronicled in this work.

It should go without saying that Jenna Plural and the Cabinet of the Solar Confederation utterly condemn the atrocities Lieutenant Dodgson claims to have participated in.

However, there are discrepancies within her tale that we can, without a doubt, refute. I shall address the two most serious accounts we know to be outright falsehoods.

Paris Sinclair did not participate in the conspiracy of Morris and Mitchell. She most certainly did not die during that event. She was, in fact, a member of the team that was down on Phobos during that event. She currently serves aboard the USS Constitution as Chief Technician.

It may be that Sinclair threatened to report several sexual harassment charges against Lieutenant Dodgson, which led to a fantasy in a very delusional mind.

On to the other matter, whilst I have already admitted in my own work and attraction to Dodgson, at no time did I act upon it. At no time that I have sexual liaisons with that woman. Even though I am a civilian, I was acting as her superior, and such an act would have been unconscionable.

Lieutenant Dodgson had a very tragic life, and the circumstances around her death will haunt many of us for a very long time.

Whilst I will never condone or excuse her actions, I would personally prefer to remember the girl with a sweet smile and what appeared to be a kind heart. The only wish of myself and Jenna Plural was that we were unable to help her.

Clear skies to you
Michael Phelkar
First Minister of Civil Affairs

A MESSAGE FROM THE AUTHOR

I really hope you enjoyed this chapter of Perceptions -
The Jenna Plural Saga.

If you would like to learn more about Jenna and the
gang, come on over to my Facebook page at www.faceb
ook.com/DavidParkerRoss, where I share nuggets about
the creation and continuation of this series. 'Like' my page,
and you will be updated and informed of new release dates
of further volumes, and special deals I have running, such
as discounts and giveaways.

Most of all, you will get to talk to me and other followers
of the saga.

However, this is not all I write. Flip over this page and
take a look at what else I've got to offer you whilst you wait
for the next installment of this series.

ALSO BY DAVID PARKER-ROSS

Space Opera - Perceptions - The Jenna Plural
Saga
Series One The Rise of Jenna
1 Jenna plural Wants You by Michael Phelkar (Available
Now)
2 That Girl from Wagga by Stacey Grant (Available Now)
3 Keeping it Semper Fi by Emma Dodgson (Jan 23)
4 Awakening of Hannah Grant by Hannah Grant (March
23)
5 The Blindside of Freedom By Bridgette Toussaint (May
23)
6 Memoir of a Martian by Abigail Thompson (July 23)
7 The Plausible Deniability Playbook by Charlotte
Kensett (Sept 23)

Fantasy Humour - The Amazon Chronicles
1 Miss Eve and the City of Men (Feb 23)

Fantasy - The Bloodline Chronicles
1 The House of Maine (April 23)

DAVID PARKER-ROSS

2 Escape from Jilrir (Aug 23)

Urban Fantasy Comedy Romance
The Rise of Artemis
(Written as DS Parker)

Made in the USA
Middletown, DE
26 November 2022